LAST
YEAR
IN
HONG
KONG

Fiction

A Kind of Treason
The Seeking
Dynasty
Manchu
Mandarin
From a Far Land
Bianca
The Everlasting Sorrow

Nonfiction

China's Red Masters
The Dragon's Seed
The Center of the World
Mao's Great Revolution
Mao vs. Chiang: The Battle for China
The Great Cities: Hong Kong
Pacific Destiny: Inside Asia Today

WILLIAM MORROW AND COMPANY, INC. / NEW YORK

LAST
YEAR
IN
HONG
KONG

A LOVE STORY

ROBERT
ELEGANT

It is the policy of William Morrow and Company, Inc., and its imprints and affiliates,
recognizing the importance of preserving what has been written, to print the books we
publish on acid-free paper, and we exert our best efforts to that end.

Library of Congress Cataloging-in-Publication Data

Elegant, Robert S.
    Last year in Hong Kong : a love story / Robert Elegant.—1st ed.
        p.   cm.   .
    ISBN 0-688-14890-5
    I. Title.
    PS3555.L37L36   1997
    813'.54—dc21   96-49003
                                                                        CIP

Printed in the United States of America

First Edition

1   2   3   4   5   6   7   8   9   10

BOOK DESIGN BY JO ANNE METSCH

For Moira, again and always,
remembering another year in Hong Kong.
And also for Victoria and Simon,
children of Hong Kong.

LAST
YEAR
IN
HONG
KONG

1

THE YOUNG MAN sat tall and proud on the gold and crimson throne, graciously bending his head so that the attendant might clasp around his neck the collar of the imperial-yellow silk robe. The bold pattern of waves on its skirts and the golden dragon coiled on its breast proclaimed him a prince of the Manchu Dynasty. The slender young woman beside him on the throne was ill at ease in the somewhat less splendid gown of an imperial concubine. She squirmed, overcome by the honor, and her feet peeped beneath her long crimson skirts.

Watching idly through the plate-glass window of the studio, Lucretia Barnes smiled. She was sympathetic, though amused. The young woman's sandals were woven of strips of shiny white plastic, and the prince had forgotten to remove his cheap digital wristwatch.

Nonetheless, the photographer appeared satisfied. Lucretia

could all but hear his thoughts under the black cloth that draped the big old-fashioned box camera. How much time could he spend on one photograph that mimicked the traditional joint portrait of a mandarin or a nobleman and his first lady in old China?

The youthful couple were recreating the past glories of the Great Empire of China. But the photographer would clear no more than two hundred fifty Hong Kong dollars, a shade more than thirty US, for the half hour it took him to coax the embarrassed couple into the pose of relaxed authority befitting their borrowed robes. Still, business was slow tonight, despite the throngs flowing through the brightly lit corridors of the pink stone building beside the terminal that served the cogwheel Peak Tram carrying holiday makers to the Peak, the highest inhabited point of Hong Kong Island.

"Guang Ming Da Jeng." A deep male voice pronounced the Chinese words meditatively, then added in crisp English, "That motto still hangs over the actual throne of the Manchus in Beijing: 'Enlightened and Just Rule!' It's an enduring illusion!"

Lucretia Barnes looked up. If he were trying to interest her, his approach was more sophisticated than the frontal assault favored by so many wealthy men in Hong Kong. She had recently fended off several such assaults. Just three days ago, a super-rich property magnate had, no more than twenty minutes after they were introduced, invited her to become his "American mistress," as he quaintly put it. The benefits of that status were breathtaking.

Of course, he'd said, she would have a five-bedroom flat staffed by two amahs and a houseboy in Crystal Mansions on the Peak—as well as a silver Rolls-Royce Corniche convertible with a uniformed chauffeur and unlimited charge accounts at Tiffany's,

Seibu, Joyce, Dunhill's, and wherever else she chose. Though her credit at Tiffany's would be limited to HK$100,000, say US$13,000, a month, he had added facetiously, she would of course be allowed to carry those monthly sums over and accumulate a far larger sum. But she would have to check with his chief secretary before taking out his 130-foot yacht.

When she declined, the billionaire had shrugged his shoulders in ostentatious indifference. But his eyes were wide with disbelief.

He knew that, since her divorce three months earlier, Lucretia Barnes had been struggling to live on the pittance the Chinese University paid her for teaching a few classes in drawing to students of architecture. He also knew that her debts were mounting, and he seriously considered buying them up. Would she then reject his offer so casually?

He was, moreover, shocked by her disdainful refusal to demand alimony from her former husband, the adroit and unscrupulous lawyer Lawrence Barnes. The shrewd speculator was convinced that Lucretia yearned after the silken luxury amid which she had so recently lived. Nor was he wholly wrong.

The man who now stood beside Lucretia outside the photographer's shop was an utterly different breed from the billionaire. This man was tentative, almost shy in his approach—if he were indeed trying to strike up an acquaintance. He did not assume that she was for sale, as almost all wealthy men, Chinese or foreign, assumed about virtually every unattached young woman in Hong Kong. However, he obviously assumed that she was educated enough to understand his reference to the old Manchu Dynasty.

Nor did his appearance conform. Certainly no more than forty years old, he wore a cream linen suit that was in its own under-stated way as assertive as the mock imperial prince's golden robe. Evidently he was not one of the men she called "black beetles" who dominated finance and commerce in Hong Kong. He did not wear the dark suit and somber tie that were the virtual uni-form of the money-mad bankers and brokers, the grasping lawyers and accountants, the market manipulators and land speculators who had transformed the Crown Colony of Hong Kong from a backwater into a flamboyant Disneyland of ostentatious wealth, at once overwhelming and, somehow, unreal.

Anyway, he did not have the look of a Hong Kong Chinese. He was too bronzed, and his nose was aquiline. His movements were too sure, his shoulders too powerful, his manner too straightforward. Nor did his eyes belong in a Chinese face: they glowed jade-green in the fluorescent light.

No, Lucretia Barnes concluded, this specimen was altogether too self-assured to be a run-of-the-mill Hong Kong male. He had an air of barbaric grandeur, as if he had come from some wild land, even from some other time.

Her curiosity was piqued. He was extraordinarily attractive, intriguing, despite her present distaste for most men—and almost all Asian men. He was even alluring, if you could apply that word to someone so strikingly masculine.

He in turn was openly assessing her, his frank gaze almost of-fensive. Yet, she sensed, his interest was untainted by either lech-ery or calculation. He might have been admiring a statue in a museum—beautiful but unobtainable.

He saw a dark-haired woman of medium height wearing red pumps that made her taller. She was, perhaps, in her early thirties, though her face was unlined and she wore no wedding ring. She was, somehow, evidently not another mindless expatriate, but a woman of individuality and intellect—quite mature and wholly in command of herself. Her expression was intent, betraying her curiosity about him. Apparently amused, she offered him a half smile.

Dorje Rabnet pulled himself up short. Recalling his responsibilities and commitments, he chided himself: This won't do, Robbie. Not at all!

How could he fantasize about a woman he would never see again? Really *should* never see again! He was all but bound to another young woman, hardly more than a girl, whom he'd seen just once—and to whom he'd never spoken a single word.

Yet his eyes did not leave this woman. She wore a gauzy violet mid-calf dress with a bodice cut square just above her breasts, yet low enough to display a necklace of sea-green jade against her matte white skin, very fair for midsummer in the subtropics. The ridiculously thin strings over her bare shoulders were, he somehow recalled, called spaghetti straps. She clutched a small black velvet purse, and a pastel-bordered Kashmir shawl lay across her arm against the frigid air conditioning she would encounter inside the building. At the moment, still outside, she was slightly flushed in the heat lingering into early evening, and her small nose was lightly dewed with perspiration.

Her eyes, a candid light blue, were cast down as if to avoid his gaze. Yet her high cheekbones and her firm chin signaled a robust character that would not shrink from confronting a challenge or an obstacle to her wishes. For coolness she had drawn her midnight-black hair back into a formal chignon. Her oval nails were cut short, but they glistened with vermilion polish.

Dorje Rabnet did not know what to make of this enigma: a

Western woman apparently alone, perhaps adrift in Asia, who looked so self-confident. Somehow, she also appeared wistful, as if frightened of missing something important, perhaps longing to know more about the outlandish corner of the world called Hong Kong. She would have to be a quick learner. Hong Kong was soon to be struck by a manmade earthquake that would shake every resident's life—personal, political, or economic. In less than a year the British Crown Colony was to pass under Beijing's control, becoming a Special Administrative Region of the People's Republic of China.

Dorje Rabnet hated the prospect. But he was resigned to it. He would have to endure in wary silence the transformation of the scattering of islands, peninsulas, and sea that had always been his home. Even if he wanted to leave, he could not.

Resigned also to never knowing this woman better, Dorje Rabnet smiled, nodded a silent farewell, and turned away. He spoke in the staccato Cantonese dialect of Hong Kong to a white-clad attendant who pointed to an escalator. Even to Lucretia Barnes, who knew only a few dozen words of Cantonese, he sounded like a native. He'd surely spoken that discordant yet highly expressive language since boyhood.

Just another Hong Kong slicker, Lucretia rebuked herself. She was through with them. British or American, European or Chinese, they were a bad lot: trivial, trifling, and grasping. Today they were more grasping than ever, as they scrabbled to grab the last possible dollar in the last years of the last boom in the boom-and-bust town that had made thousands of millionaires, hundreds of multimillionaires, and a handful of billionaires.

Dorje Rabnet turned and nodded hesitantly again, strangely unsure of himself. Lucretia Barnes nodded politely in return. He turned away and stepped onto the escalator. A little puzzled, she put the chance encounter out of her mind.

LUCRETIA DABBED HER forehead with a lace handkerchief and threw the Kashmir shawl over her shoulders before stepping into the chilly elevator. Yet she shivered when she entered the fiercely air-conditioned Café Deco where whirlpools of tobacco smoke swirled.

Though few women in Hong Kong or China smoked at all, Chinese men of Hong Kong, like their cousins in China, smoked compulsively. Not that they were deliberately defying death. Nor were they suicidal. It was more complex, their love of the poison weed. As if they knew that past indulgence had already condemned them to early death and they were now wringing every possible pleasure—including the deadly pleasure of tobacco—out of their remaining days. Such fatalistic addiction matched the mood and decor of the café, which looked across the fairyland lights of the harbor toward incandescent Kowloon on the far shore. The café's furnishings dated back to the thirties and forties, when smoking was dashing and glamorous, long before killjoy scientists labeled it harmful.

The glass tops of the cocktail tables rested on old Manhattan elevator dials. Songs popular three quarters of a century earlier gushed from the gaudy Wurlitzer jukebox beside the minute dance floor. All shining glass and polished steel, the jukebox threw off purple, red, and silver rays. The highly polished oak bar on the other side of the dance floor had come from a New York speakeasy, and the silver cocktail shakers had been battered by hard use.

Lucretia paused beside the bar to savor the orgy of nostalgia created by the tough little Sardinian proprietor, then pulled herself away. At the head of the voluptuously curved internal staircase, she saw a placard in a chromium stand announcing: HONG KONG SOCIETY OF ARCHITECTS—ANNUAL DINNER MEETING 1996.

She should have been at ease. Most of the architects were old acquaintances. Some were even friends. Yet she was embarrassed; she had not been able to raise the HK$800 admission fee. Without telling her, her friends had chipped in to buy her a ticket. Once they'd surprised her with it, she had no choice but to go. The ticket cost hardly more than US$100, which was no longer trifling to Lucretia.

That sum had been no more than a generous tip to an attentive hairdresser when she was married to Lawrence Barnes. He was accustomed to buying popularity—or, at least, obsequious service—by strewing largesse around him like a Saudi prince on a spree. The habit of lavishness was easy to pick up, but it was hard to break now, when her marriage was behind her.

Teaching at the Chinese University had originally been something of a lark, as well as a window onto the reality of everyday life in Hong Kong, from which her own opulent manner of life set her apart. She had taught for the joy of using her talents fully, as well as the pleasure of passing her skills on to eager students. Teaching was now a grim necessity, though the stipend barely kept her afloat.

Lucretia was also ill at ease being on her own. It was as if she'd gone back to another time, another place, when a woman was incomplete—almost indecent—without a man at her side. Her mother's strict code of behavior had decreed: *A lady does not attend a public dinner unescorted!* But there was no man she would have wanted to escort her. She wondered again whether she should have come at all.

Cambridge, where she was born, was once known with its neighbor Boston as the Athens of America. Old inhabitants and newcomers alike were fiercely progressive in politics and outlook. The People's Republic of Cambridge, many called it, not entirely in jest. But old Cambridge families, both the genteel poor and the discreetly rich, were socially conservative. Ostentatiously modest, the old guard shunned display. Lucretia's ancestors had held to the credo: *Rigorous thinking and plain living.* That was just as well, as her father sometimes remarked, since nowadays the family did not have a red cent to spend for either show or luxury.

Her family could find just enough money to bring her home if she were desperate. Yet what would she do in Cambridge? Rust away like a spinster aunt in an uninspiring, wholly predictable environment?

But the family could hardly find enough for her to live, however modestly, in hyperexpensive Hong Kong. Could not and would not if it could! She was weighing in her mind the question of leaving Hong Kong. Of course she'd never ask the family for help. What, her father would demand, could she possibly want in that outlandish place that was not available in Cambridge, except perhaps a wildly extravagant lifestyle?

Hong Kong's wealthy families, as the gossip columnist of the South China Morning Post repeatedly observed, now asked themselves, "What's the good of a fortune if you don't flaunt it?" The super-rich loved to parade their wealth. Long gone were the days when it was considered the height of quirky extravagance to dye a poodle pink to match its mistress's pink-dyed hair and pink-painted Rolls-Royce. Much greater excess was now commonplace.

Indeed, the concept of extravagance was virtually unknown to the new super-rich. It was not unusual for them to buy a diamond necklace for, say, US$1.8 million on impulse or to charter jumbo jets to bring relations, friends, and business associates from the ends of the earth for a weekend party. Even after years of associating with the super-rich while married to Lawrence, Lucretia was still taken aback by their ostentation and their sheer bad taste. Yet she was no bluenose to condemn all pleasure. She could relish the inspired fantasy of the Café Deco even though her New England conscience nagged a little.

She found a chair at a long table kept for late arrivals, not noticing until she was served that the barrister H. K. Lam was seated nearby. She detested Lam. Like her ex-husband, he was a jackal of the property speculators, always eager to lead those lions to their prey. After the kill, he would happily gorge himself on the bloody scraps. She nodded distantly and turned away without speaking.

As always at the café, the food was very good, though the enormous servings were too much of a good thing: crispy smoked-pigeon spring rolls with sweet chili garlic followed by Thai braised pig knuckles and three desserts. Satiated, Lucretia dutifully listened to the bombastic after-dinner speeches. Their style was flamboyant, their theme the same. Architect after architect congratulated himself and, incidentally, his colleagues for transforming Hong Kong into an awesome metropolis of marble, steel, and glass towers.

Lucretia's head drooped, but she pulled herself erect. Wearisome speeches on top of heavy food were lulling.

Yet she suddenly knew she wanted to stay in Hong Kong, despite her musing about leaving the Colony. She wanted to stay because she had fallen in love with the other Hong Kong, what little she knew of it, which was a workaday home for millions, rather than a playground for a few thousand super-rich.

She had glimpsed that everyday Hong Kong when her students or her colleagues momentarily drew aside the curtain that normally concealed their world from her. That other Hong Kong was made up of men and women who toiled for their daily rice, men and women who aspired and strove. Many were moved by aesthetic and intellectual issues that the wealthy predators and wastrels at the top never knew or disdained as tomfoolery because neither art nor literature produced immediate material rewards.

She also wanted to see what would become of the people of Hong Kong under a Communist regime. Though it constantly proclaimed its overriding concern for the masses, that regime constantly abused the masses in China. Perhaps she could, somehow, fight for more freedom for the people. She knew herself too well to believe she would not, perhaps, veer from that purpose. Indeed, she might well change her mind again about remaining after the People's Liberation Army marched in. That could be perilous. Yet Hong Kong was suddenly very dear to her.

But how could she stay? For that matter, the question was whom among the hundreds of thousands of resident foreigners the Communists would permit to stay. Anyway, she couldn't stay unless she found new sources of income.

Lucretia heard the forced Oxford accent of H. K. Lam and

realized that he was talking to her. He was sarcastic and cutting—as he had been since she rebuffed his advances some years ago. "Well now, Mrs. Barnes, I suppose you'll be scuttling soon. Of course, Lawrence is staying—and he'll be very welcome. But people like you, the naysayers and the saboteurs, should scurry."

Lucretia remembered that the barrister was not only a jackal of the property speculators, but a senior member of Beijing's puppet Preparatory Commission for the Special Administrative Region of Hong Kong. The Communists had packed the Commission with local well-to-do sympathizers and opportunists so as to put a gloss of popular approval on the takeover. The same yes-men were later to elect an even smaller group to select the territory's new Chief Executive. That was true democracy, the Communists were saying, not the pretense of democracy offered at the last minute by the British. For the first time the voice of Hong Kong's people would be heard in the choice of a governor. But Lucretia knew the Communists were the ventriloquists.

Most ordinary people, the exploited masses, as Beijing would say, were bitterly opposed to Communist rule. Several elections had made their wishes unmistakable: *Let the British stay!* But their wishes counted for nothing against the deal London believed it had made: surrendering Hong Kong in return for much greater British trade with China.

Lucretia ignored Lam's gratuitous insult. Lawrence had told her that Lam aspired to be Chief Justice of the Special Administrative Region. Eager to please the new overlords, he made it his mission to drive out "unsuitable foreigners." That meant anyone with an independent outlook. It was odd: The capitalist exploiters, once fiercely denounced by Beijing, by and large supported the authoritarian Communists, while the common people, the exploited masses, wanted to keep the new democracy that the British had tardily introduced.

"Cat got your tongue, my dear Lucretia?" Lam pressed. "No bright answer?"

"It's not your business, Counselor Lam, whether I go or stay," Lucretia replied softly. "And I'm not your Lucretia, dear or otherwise."

"Certainly not," he agreed smoothly. "Nor anyone else's dear anything, I've noticed. . . . So you're planning to stay on as long as the pickings are good?"

"Assume what you will, Counselor." She knew her sweet tone would irritate him. "Perhaps I'll stay to see how *you* make out. It'll suit you just fine, won't it? Scavenging, picking up others' leavings."

"We don't need bloody-minded foreigners . . . outsiders like you. And we certainly don't need foreign tarts!" Lam's face purpled, and his eyes bulged. "We know how to handle big-nosed, white-skinned parasites!"

"So you're a racist, as well as a running dog of the Communists!" Lucretia finally erupted. "And a fool—"

She broke off abruptly and turned her back to the barrister. Lam would be further enraged by her studied disregard.

Her gaze swept the smoky meeting room and met the jade-green eyes she had seen earlier outside the photographer's shop. Those eyes were frankly appraising her again. The man in the cream linen suit, whom she'd already dismissed from her thoughts, was seated at an adjoining table. Hearing her voice raised, he had swiveled around to stare at her.

To her intense annoyance, Lucretia flushed like a schoolgirl. She believed that she had concealed her fury at Lam from the others in the café. But she could not conceal her indignation at the green eyes' appraising her as if she stood on the block at a slave auction.

She was somehow afraid of that man, fearful of her own impulsiveness as well. She had met Lawrence Barnes one instant, loved him the next, and married him just a week later. Although it had lasted almost three years, their marriage, was a disaster from the beginning. She had, however, learned the lesson well: she was perilously susceptible to a certain kind of masculine charm.

Yet this man was not the kind who normally attracted her. He was a little too handsome, too self-assured. He looked too much like an idealized portrait of a noble Iroquois: dark, strong-featured, always master of himself, and wholly at ease in the world.

Was he, she wondered, as self-satisfied as he appeared? Any man who looked so striking and carried himself so proudly must surely be self-centered and arrogant. Was he as domineering, she wondered, as his manner suggested?

Still seething from her encounter with Lam, she was irritated by this man's unwavering gaze and his knowing smile. She smiled coolly in return, happy that she would never learn what he was really like. She would never get that close to him.

As if in response to her musings, he rose and took the vacant chair beside her. She could not object. All present were assumed to be colleagues—and were encouraged to get to know each other better. At least, his presence would keep H. K. Lam from renewing the quarrel. She realized belatedly that he had deliberately come to her rescue, and she was grateful.

"My name's Rabnet, Dorje Rabnet." His accent was English and educated; unlike Lam's accent, it was not pretentious. "Most people call me Robbie."

"Do they!" she said. "Why tell me?"

Her tone was not neutral, as she'd meant it to be, but cold, even antagonistic. Well, she wanted to discourage him, and she would—no matter how thick his skin.

He asked, "What've I done to you? Why snap at me?"

Taken aback, Lucretia smiled tautly. "Since you ask, I'll tell you. I just let go at you after putting up with that . . . that insufferable boor."

"Why me?" he persisted.

"If you must know, I'm beginning to dislike Asian men. You're obviously Asian and a man—and you got in the line of fire."

Dorje Rabnet was irritated, his first instinct to get up and leave. This imperious American woman did not have a monopoly on either pride or sensitivity. Yet he was intrigued, and he repeated, "Dorje Rabnet, mostly called Robbie."

"What an extraordinary name!" She relented slightly. "Where's it from?"

"Tibet. But I'm a Hong Kong boy, born and bred."

"You don't look Tibetan."

Lucretia knew that remark was just silly. She had not forgotten that she meant to discourage him. But she was drawn by his candor, his readiness to confide in a stranger.

"Tibetan on my father's side," he said. "My mother's as English as Yorkshire pudding. But don't ever tell her I said so. She hates the stuff."

Lucretia bridled. How could he blandly assume that she would get to know his family? Anyway he was, at least, enlivening this dreary meeting.

"Why do they call you Robbie?" She told herself she was prolonging the conversation to keep him beside her as a shield against H. K. Lam.

"It started when I was at Imperial College in London. My classmates christened me Robbie . . . from Rabnet, my family name. And Dorje . . . you mustn't laugh . . . Dorje means Thunderbolt."

She did laugh at that, no longer resenting his questioning, and she realized that she'd performed an emotional somersault. Nonetheless, Dorje Rabnet was of no interest to her as a male. He was merely an interesting human being whose impetuous confidences were charming and disarming, also a little disconcerting.

"Who are you now?" She meant to be as straightforward, as provoking as he was. "You must be terribly important, a big-shot architect. Who else would dare wear that wonderful linen suit, like something out of the nineteen-fifties? You're certainly not a black beetle!"

"Black beetle?"

"All those ridiculously proper men in their neat little dark suits! Shysters, land grabbers, and money shufflers, all licensed to steal. I call them black beetles."

Robbie smiled, then replied soberly, "No, I'm certainly not one of your black beetles. I'm not at all important, either."

"Nonsense!" she retorted. "Don't be so modest."

"Really, I'm just a chap with an ordinary low-paid nine-to-five job. And the suit . . . it's the only one I've got except for a blue serge number that's as heavy and as rigid as sheet iron. Good for London, guaranteed to wear forever—until it's as shiny as a mirror. Also guaranteed to turn into a puddle of grease anyone who wears it in the Hong Kong summer."

"I see!" Lucretia chuckled deep in her throat. "And what's this job of yours?"

"I'm a civil engineer. I've been trained to design bridges and roads, buildings, too. Right now I'm only proofing other men's designs, so—" He broke off, then said, "You know all about me, but I don't even know your name."

"I'm Lucretia . . ."

She paused, startled to find herself on the verge of exchanging confidences. She certainly would not tell him her entire history on first acquaintance. Nor would she ever talk about her divorce. "Lucretia . . . Barnes . . . I suppose." She disliked using her former husband's name. "I'm not an architect either, only a painter. But I do teach budding architects—drawing, perspective, and so on. They're wonderful students, the best I've ever had, eager and quick to learn, diligent and idealistic. But afterward, when they graduate, they're disastrous . . . disgraceful!"

Robbie wondered why she'd hesitated before saying, "Barnes." And why had she added, "I suppose"? But he didn't probe.

"Disastrous? Disgraceful?" he asked instead. "That's strong language."

"Not at all! Just look what they inflict on us when they become practicing architects! Those great slab-sided skyscrapers . . ." She was fluent and eloquent, almost as if she'd expressed those strong sentiments a number of times before. ". . . hideous monuments to the monumental egos of the property magnates! Have you ever looked at the Central Plaza Building?"

"What's wrong with it? It works, doesn't it?"

"In a competition for the world's most tasteless building, the Central Plaza would surely be a finalist. That stubby pinnacle with the enormous long needle of a spire defying Heaven itself. And at night the gaudy spotlights on its fat gilt flanks . . . the green glare shrieking for attention. It's downright atrocious."

"I don't expect beauty. As long as a building works, fulfills its purpose."

"So you're an old fashioned utilitarian . . . form follows function and all that guff!" she responded. "What about the new Bank of China building? Old I. M. Pei, the master architect, made it domineering and threatening—and deliberately ugly. A knife in the heart of Hong Kong, the people call it!"

"It fulfills its purpose, even if you don't like that purpose," he insisted. "It's meant to symbolize Beijing's power and Beijing's sovereignty over Hong Kong. So it does! What more can one ask?"

"We can damn well demand—demand, not ask—that these buildings make our surroundings more attractive . . . more human. Downtown Hong Kong stifles the human spirit, all the way from Central to Wanchai and Causeway Bay. And the apartment towers on the hills, they're downright deadening."

Robbie suppressed his smile at her vehemence. So many sparks were flying between them, and he was afraid she would erupt again if she thought he was mocking her. He did not know what he wanted from this impassioned woman. But it was definitely not a quarrel.

"Now's no time for grace notes," he declared. "Good solid structures for shelter, convenient places to work and live. That's what's needed."

"A building, a neighborhood, can be so much more. It can nourish, exalt, the human spirit, instead of—" Lucretia clapped a hand over her mouth. "I'm talking too much!"

"Not at all. It's fascinating. Tell me, what do you propose to do about this terrible ugliness you see all around you?"

"Hong Kong has to do what they do in Germany. Three percent of the cost of a new building has to go for works of art—statues in open places or shopping malls. Also murals and mosaics. Art shows us we're human, not just machines for producing and consuming wealth—or operating all the crazy gadgets we've invented. Human, at least. Maybe even a touch of the divine."

"Enforcing that rule would be devilish." He was feeling his way, determinedly honest though he did not want to antagonize her. "And I can't see such little touches having much impact."

"Let me show you," she offered impulsively. "Let me show you Edinburgh Court!"

RIDING DOWN THE Peak Tram and then climbing Garden Road to her room at the YWCA, which she couldn't really afford, Lucretia wondered why she was bothering with Dorje Rabnet. He was so matter-of-fact, so prosaic, so totally unromantic. Maybe that was it, the attraction of opposites. She was impetuous and fanciful, sometimes far too sentimental, and often impractical.

Still thinking about Dorje Rabnet, she was suddenly appalled by her slanging match with H. K. Lam. He was disgusting, subhuman, a slavering jackal, a carrion crow. Still, she should not have allowed him to enrage her. Two years ago, she would simply have brushed him off, ignored him. But her temper was uncertain nowadays. She herself could not predict at one moment what she might say the next. She was ashamed of—and a little alarmed at—her lightning shifts of mood.

It was now three months since she had been legally severed from Lawrence Barnes. It was well over a year since she had begun to think of divorce, wrestling all the while with her New England conscience. She was still haunted by a sense of guilt and, even worse, a feeling of inadequacy. Three months after the formal divorce, she was still riding an emotional roller coaster, swooping down to anger and soaring to enthusiasm for her new independence, then down again to near-despair—all in a few moments. So it was, too, with her wavering from determination to remain in Hong Kong after Beijing took over to the conviction that she must get away.

Would she ever feel like herself again? And—would she ever be able to love anyone again? And why did she ask herself that question?

WHILE LUCRETIA TRUDGED toward the YWCA, Dorje Rabnet entered the small restaurant where he often ate. He wanted to pick up the meaty bones they saved for his small dog, a dictatorial shih-tzu called Jacobus. But his thoughts wandered elsewhere. Was he losing his stability, he wondered, even his purpose?

Considering his delicate position, the last thing he should do was get involved with a woman like Lucretia Barnes. She was too intelligent, far too attractive—and she'd struck him like a blow. She challenged him as few woman had in all his thirty-nine years. Dedicated and outspoken, clear-sighted and honest, she could be dangerous.

It would be foolhardy, even reckless, to pursue this woman. He would, besides, be trifling with the emotions of the girl-woman to whom he was half-betrothed. He would also be betraying the trust of those closest to him.

Nonetheless he would meet her and see Edinburgh Court. Just this once, he swore. After that it would be all over.

2

ROBBIE HAD ALIGHTED from the red bus in front of the low white buildings of the Country Club, which shone in the late morning sunshine like a fortress in fairyland. Now it was all uphill, the walk at least. Shouson Hill Road was getting steeper as he climbed the road.

He found himself whistling the jaunty tune that had been a favorite of his mother. How did the chorus go? Something about God not making little green apples and it not raining in Indianapolis in the summertime. He liked that sprightly irreverence, and he often caught himself whistling that tune when he was light-hearted—or sometimes for no reason at all. Today, however, he knew precisely why.

This Friday in mid-August he had unashamedly taken time off work for the first time in years. He was clad in a Madras sports shirt and white cotton trousers. In his Gucci-style moccasins with golden horse-bits across the instep and his racy Ray-Ban aviator sunglasses, he felt dashing and free. That garb was utterly different from the rough work clothes he wore on construction sites or the jackets and ties required in the office. This was a new Dorje Rabnet.

Lucretia Barnes was waiting for him at Edinburgh Mansions at the top of Shouson Hill. The morning was even brighter for the promise of that meeting.

Yet there was really no promise at all, neither stated nor implied. He was nonetheless exhilarated. Yet he was determined that their meeting must lead nowhere. Still, the mere thought of seeing her again very soon filled him with delight. He hurried uphill with long easy strides, by exaltation uplifted.

Should he ever tread the road to Nirvana, the ultimate Buddhist Heaven, he would feel just as he did at this minute. He would feel again this joyous fizzing in his blood; he would be bathed in the unearthly radiance of this crystalline light. Of course, those who finally attained Nirvana were already disembodied, virtually depersonated. They, the elect, had already cast aside all earthly desire, whether for power, for riches, or for beauty, whether it be manmade or naturemade. They had, above all, cast off the desire for love, earthly or spiritual.

Robbie smiled in rueful self-mockery. What exalted notions! He was certainly *not* beyond desire, not totally mature. Quite the contrary, he felt much younger than thirty-nine, perhaps an avid seventeen or eighteen with idealism and hormones raging against each other in his blood.

At sixteen he had learned about dating. The kids at the Island School were already going out on dates, chiefly the Americans, but also some English and French, as well as the rich Western-oriented Chinese. But dating was not for him, a minority within a minority. A Eurasian was acceptable to the still tolerant young-sters, though even they found the Tibetan strain outlandish. But a Eurasian lacking a wealthy and powerful father, lacking any visible father at all, was mocked by teenagers who had been taught by their ambitious parents to be acutely status-conscious.

The light on Shouson Hill dimmed as if a soiled rag had been dragged across the sun, and Robbie suddenly felt much older. Strange to feel eighteen one moment and ancient the next! His own confusion finally came home to him. How could he rejoice at meeting Lucretia one moment and the next swear he would never see her again after this day?

Robbie sensed an automobile creeping toward him. It was vir-tually silent, a rakish fire-engine-red Rolls-Royce moving very slowly.

When the Rolls drew level with him, the rear window slid down. A bony liver-spotted hand at the end of a dark-gray sleeve beckoned imperiously. Robbie leaned into the window and saw against the cream leather upholstery the slight figure of T. Y. Lee, proprietor and chief executive of the Bank of Ningpo and Fuchow. The banker was an old friend of his mother.

"Good morning, Dorje." Relentlessly formal, old T. Y. Lee never called him Robbie. "I see you're taking your morning con-stitutional. Thank God, I'm too old for this fad of exercise."

The old man, eighty-five if he was a day, had been to King's College when the University of Cambridge was still an enclave of great privilege—and had lived as opulently as any English gran-dee. His mellow Cambridge accent was as authentic as H. K. Lam's Oxford accent, but was not colored by Lam's pretension and condescension. T. Y. Lee had been at Cambridge as a right.

He had been lavishly maintained by his old-monied family, while H. K. Lam had had to claw his way up. Though the two were different in almost every way, a waggish colonial secretary had once dubbed them Tweedlelam and Tweedlelee. So they remained to most old British residents.

T. Y. could only conclude that Robbie was walking for exercise. The old man could not believe that one of his own class was walking uphill simply to reach the top. It was equally inconceivable to him that economic need should press the son of an old friend.

Why not, he might ask, take your car and chauffeur? Or drive yourself if the chauffeur's on his day off? He himself kept four chauffeurs, one for each eight hours of the twenty-four, the fourth as a spare and for Sundays.

"A very good morning, Uncle Lee!" T. Y. Lee's elaborate old-fashioned courtesy required a reply in kind. He was uncle to Robbie as an old friend of the family who had gotten Robbie admitted to Imperial College and had paid the bills.

"I'm delighted to see you looking so sprightly," Robbie added. "You know, you really should try exercising, even—"

"Nonsense, my boy," the light voice interjected. "It would undoubtedly kill me. . . . And how is your dear mother?"

"As well as can be, sir. Yesterday, she seemed to remember who I was for a moment."

Robbie played it T. Y. Lee's way. The old man insisted that Althea Garland Rabnet would soon recover from Alzheimer's disease and leave the Hong Kong Sanatorium.

"You'll see, Dorje," he said. "She'll be right as rain in a month or two. Back with you in your tiny house."

T. Y. Lee was playing his little game of pretending all was as it had once been, pretending he did not know that Robbie had years ago sold the oddly named Small House on Old Peak Road, where he had been reared. A massive block of apartments now stood where the small house and its large garden had once been. The proceeds of that sale, carefully invested, were keeping his mother in the Sanatorium. But Robbie had to draw on the capital from time to time, as well as making a sizable contribution from his salary every month. He could not ask his Uncle Lee for help with the bills. He'd already taken too much from the old man.

How often he wished he hadn't sold the Small House for a few hundred thousand Hong Kong dollars. It would bring HK$25 million today, more if a speculative builder were desperate to put up a fifty-five-story block of flats.

That sum, more than US$3 million, could have changed his life substantially. But not entirely. He had no desire to be a playboy. He was happy with his work—and would never change it voluntarily. Anyway, the hypothetical money was gone for good.

Every member of the middle class who had been in the Colony a few decades ago felt his own regrets: either for selling property too soon or for failing to buy soon enough. Old T. Y. Lee had no such regrets, having taken highly profitable action shortly before every major development.

Yet he often talked as if nothing had changed in the Colony since the sleepy nineteen-fifties. The octogenarian wasn't really befuddled. He still knew every significant event almost before it happened. But it pleased him to talk as if Hong Kong and its people had passed unchanged through the most turbulent and most fruitful decades of their lives.

T. Y. Lee's small eyes, just visible amid the crow's feet, glinted in the dimness of the Rolls. He said, "By the way, my boy, a word of advice."

"I value your advice, sir." The shrewd old man was genuinely concerned for Robbie's welfare—and he wielded great power in the Colony. "It's not a tip on the stock market, is it? I could use one."

"Rubbish, Dorje. You know as much as anyone about the property market, maybe more. You could make a killing if you'd only use your information."

"Insider's knowledge, Uncle Lee, which—"

"Everyone knows it's shady, maybe illegal," the old man interjected. "But everyone exploits insider's knowledge."

"I know insiders're always buying and selling on the back of privileged information—stealing from the small investor but unscathed. I'd get caught. I've got no backup, no network of crooked friends behind me. Out there alone, I'd be very vulnerable."

"Yes, you are vulnerable. All the more reason to be careful."

"Careful, sir?"

"Careful about whom you associate with. Now this Mrs. Barnes you were so cozy with the other night, I'd stay away from her if I were you."

Robbie shook his head and protested, "We only chatted for half an hour or so. Nothing else."

"And you're only quick-marching up Shouson Hill to meet her right now, aren't you? I caught a glimpse of her at Edinburgh Mansions. She looked expectant."

"Expectant, sir? I'm not guilty, only met her a day ago."

"A lame joke, my boy. You are meeting her, aren't you?"

"Yes, I am, sir." Robbie felt like a schoolboy caught in a lie.

Only the old banker could make him cringe that way. "But only to look at a few statues and paintings."

"Asked you up to see her etchings, has she? It's gone farther than I thought." A wry smile twisted the old man's thin lips. "You must not let it go any farther, Dorje."

"Why not, sir?"

"Associating with Lucretia Barnes is bound to affect your reputation . . . and your work. She's not fond of our coming rulers, and her tongue is constantly running away with her. Not that she may not be right, mind you."

The old man paused in reflection and then said, "What's more, her former husband, that rascal Lawrence Barnes, is sucking up to Beijing. He's saying she's a dangerous agitator . . . who wants to resist Beijing's lawful authority. He denounces her as a right-wing radical.

"Now those jumped-up peasants from Beijing, our future overlords, they're not going to sift evidence or hold jury trials. She's already suspect—and anyone suspect is for the chop. Buzz around Ms. Lucretia Barnes like a bee around a honeypot—and you'll be suspect, too. You'll be for the chop along with her. Meanwhile, they won't let you into China to check on your clients' new buildings."

"I'd been thinking along the same lines about her . . . about Lucretia." Robbie did no more than tell the truth. "I'll probably never see her again after today."

"Sordid, Dorje, damned sordid. No gentleman should be put in such a position, certainly no lady. But they're not gentlemen or ladies, our future overlords."

T. Y. Lee shook his head. "A great pity! A lady mixed up in dirty politics. . . . Besides, she's a damned attractive girl!"

The sentiments were Edwardian, as was the tone. He pronounced the words much as Robbie's maternal great-grandmother would have: "A demned ettretive gel."

THE FIRE-ENGINE-red Rolls pulled away, and Robbie started uphill again. He had not reacted to T. Y. Lee's acid asides on the Communists, for he had to appear neutral, even with his mentor. Otherwise, he would imperil his other work, which he never discussed. Yet that work would have been open and aboveboard if anyone other than the paranoid Beijing regime were concerned.

The old gentleman, who was rarely wrong, had reinforced Robbie's own fears regarding Lucretia. But T. Y. Lee did not know about that further complication, the promised bride, the girl-woman, for that was still solely between Tibetans. Robbie trudged uphill despondently.

An instant later his spirits soared. Around the tree-bordered curve he glimpsed the green marble gateposts of Edinburgh Mansions, which was a complex of apartment houses, shops, and schools. Just inside the tall iron gates capped with gilt spearheads stood a woman in an orange dress and a big straw hat, who was chatting with the red-bearded Pathan guards. It was Lucretia Barnes.

Robbie astonished himself. He had not felt so strongly about a woman since London. In his mid-twenties and still naive, he had found the straightforward and experimental English girls an endless delight. He'd been constantly in love during those three years—or so he'd believed.

But the sight of Lucretia made his memories of other women fade. His heart leaped. Hard to believe this was only their second meeting—and their first had been no more than twenty-odd minutes of desultory chat.

When she turned to greet him, he saw that her breasts lolled provocatively in the halter top of her backless sundress. He clasped both her hands, which she impulsively extended. She wore very little makeup. Her mouth, which had been a vivid red peony the other night, was now barely tinted. Still, her full lips were arresting against her matte white skin. Her light-blue eyes were framed by a touch of liner, but her oval nails were free of polish. Her raven's wing hair, shining blue-black in the sunshine, was plaited in a long braid that hung down her bare back. She looked eighteen, at most twenty.

"Hello, Thunderbolt!" She smiled broadly. "All charged up for our big debate?"

"Is it meant to be a debate? I thought it was a friendly discussion."

"Afraid to debate me?" she challenged. "And you're called Thunderbolt!"

"Dorje also means solid and dependable," he said with mock solemnity. "I'm here for a peaceful talk, not a hot debate."

"Well, if that's what you want . . ."

Today, she was lighthearted and humorous, open and warm, no longer prickly and defensive as she'd been at the Café Deco. Yet she was probably trying to charm him into endorsing her all but religious devotion to art. She could not possibly feel as he did: ensnared by tenderness, ambushed by joy.

"You should know," Robbie began conscientiously, "that I'm not an architect. What's more, I'm—"

"I know," Lucretia broke in. "You told me the other evening at the Deco. So what?"

"Now, you . . ."

Unthinking, he rubbed his knuckles across his eyes. Catching himself, he dropped his hand to his side. Had she also caught his self-deprecating gesture?

" . . . you should know I work for Granger, Reynolds, and O'Dowd, chartered surveyors. We examine architects' specifications before construction. A civil engineer's needed to assess the load-bearing structure. We also check costs and workmanship of buildings, bridges, and docks for safety and durability. . . . I'm not a partner, only an employee. Why waste your time with me?"

"Robbie, you told me all this before. Beats me what we call a chartered surveyor in the States. Probably a certified appraiser of major structures. Anyway, something grandiose . . ."

She had almost said "appraiser of erections," had caught herself just in time. An earthy wench with a broad sense of humor, a throwback perhaps to some ancestor who was a court lady in the bawdy Elizabethan era, sometimes peeped out from her virtuous New England facade. Not often, Lucretia reflected, but occasionally. She was a passionate woman who loved to laugh, as well as a daughter of the Puritans. Born in the middle of the tumultuous sixties, she was also a daughter of that permissive, licentious, and sensual era.

"Whatever . . ." she added. "Please let me decide when I'm wasting my time."

Had she been too forward? She did not want to frighten away this unassuming yet dazzlingly attractive man who was so oddly called Thunderbolt. His sensitivity to her feelings, his modesty—though modesty could be overdone—and his stunning looks had struck her like a thunderbolt. He was, besides, blessedly free of the usual Hong Kong hypocrisy and greed. Above all, he was secure, comfortable with his place in the world. That was his greatest attraction.

His strength, his self-assurance, were just what she needed. She was not looking for a breadwinner or a sugar daddy. She could always manage to feed and clothe herself—and she could easily do without diamonds or sables. But she needed a champion to keep her safe while she regained her own self-confidence.

Lucretia was already reconsidering her impulsive decision to remain in Hong Kong, not just for another month or two, but for some time after the Communists took over. She was still drifting, unable to make a firm decision. *To stay or to go?* she asked herself. *If to stay, for how long? If to go, where?*

Was Robbie enough to keep her here? Hard to say on such brief acquaintance. After the first glorious shock of meeting a man she could love, a woman always wondered if there could develop enduring affection on which, perhaps, to build a new life. But that question was premature, merely fantasizing with so little to go on.

"Anyway," she repeated, "*I'll* decide who's wasting my time, if you please!"

"Sorry!" Robbie was not fazed. "Of course, it's entirely up to you what you do with your time. Though I'd like to take up some of it."

She registered the compliment, but did not respond. "Look, Robbie, I'm no great shakes in Hong Kong, either. I don't even know whether I'll still be here next week or next month."

Robbie should have been pleased at her hinting that she could soon leave. Once gone, she would no longer imperil his work or his emotional stability. Obviously, it was foolhardy to pay her attention that might keep her. Yet at the thought of her leaving, his face fell, and Lucretia added reassuringly, "There're also lots to keep me here, you know. Painting and sculpture could be wondrous again in East Asia. Look at the impact of Buddhist art over the centuries."

She was clearly fascinated by the subject, not just talking to impress him.

"Asia's growing far too fast," she said. "Everyone's too busy expanding and consuming. They forget that human beings don't live by bread—or rice—alone. Not only the body, but the spirit must be nourished—by art, as well as prayer."

She paused, suddenly self-conscious, then asked, "But who am I to talk? I know a tiny bit about Hong Kong . . . very superficially. Who am I to lecture you on Hong Kong or Asia?"

Had she, Lucretia wondered, enticed Robbie by falsely pretending it was only his opinion on art in architecture she valued? She did truly want his opinion. He was open-minded, not smug and closed-minded like the money crowd she had been running with. He took his profession seriously, and it was a practical nuts-and-bolts profession. If she could convince him, there really was hope for the campaign to beautify Hong Kong. But she wanted, needed, much more from Robbie than such support.

"Anyway, I asked you here to look at the art work," she said aloud. "I'll show you the worst part first. Hong Kong taste can be wacky, lurid, disastrous. So many care only for money."

"That's not quite so, Lucretia! Yes, Hong Kong started that way with opium smuggling. But there've always been those who care about education, literature, music, and art. We're not all money-grubbers."

"I haven't seen them," she replied brusquely. "Where are they all hiding, your artists and their patrons?"

"You wouldn't see them, not where you were hanging out . . .

on the Peak with your head in the clouds. Come down to earth and I'll show you *my* Hong Kong, the real Hong Kong."

"I'd like that," she agreed. "I've only had a glimpse or two of that Hong Kong."

"Just keep your eyes open," he advised, "and . . . forget your preconceptions."

He had almost said "and keep your mouth shut." Having begun an impersonal—or, at least, detached—discussion, they were both growing heated. He almost welcomed that sudden rancor between them; it could help get him off the hook of her attraction. But he was also horrified.

Were they, Lucretia wondered, verging on a quarrel about an abstract issue? Was their mutual attraction also creating friction? She tried to turn the dispute around. "Whatever, it's all politics and horse trading now, isn't it? What happens next, I mean, the disaster for Hong Kong after the Communists take over."

"Possibly, though I don't see it quite that way."

Robbie hated equivocating, but his true opinion was too close to hers. As T. Y. Lee had warned, he had to avoid being identified with Lucretia's fierce views. Her dossier in Beijing was undoubtedly marked *fanhua,* literally "anti-Chinese," which meant an enemy of the Communists. He simply could not afford to be labeled *fanhua.*

"Besides, the Colony's past isn't all greed and ostentation. Hong Kong gave me a good education at almost no cost, and I'm deeply grateful. Hong Kong's given education and opportunity, thus dignity, to millions of poor girls and boys. It's not just financial monkey business, showy spending, and hard-drinking foreigners."

"Sometimes you sound smug," Lucretia riposted. "Is Hong Kong really so kind and generous? Not from the little I've seen."

"Just wait till you've seen more before you pronounce judgment."

It was high time to end this discussion. Personal antagonism was springing from their disagreement. Lucretia rarely felt anger at someone she did not care about unless she was deliberately provoked, as she had been by H. K. Lam's insults. But she could get very angry at someone she really cared about.

"Anyway," she said, "let's have a look at Edinburgh Mansions."

High and blank, like a passage in the Forbidden City in Beijing, the red-veined marble walls of the central building were at once majestic and mysterious. Above the green marble entrance shone a ten-foot-high gilt thistle, the emblem of Scotland. Edinburgh Mansions must have been named by some homesick Scot or some native son of Hong Kong who had studied in Scotland. Hong Kong was great for instant tradition.

Just short of the marble entrance, Lucretia turned into a narrow passage that led to a Roman amphitheater: a half-bowl with tiers of white marble benches looking down on a half-Olympic swimming pool. A pair of sleek women in skimpy racing suits, one blonde and the other Chinese, splashed back and forth in fast crawls, working hard to make themselves even sleeker.

"They really flipped on this one." Lucretia pointed to the marble statues that stood on the rear parapet of the amphitheater. "Sort of post-modern Graeco-Roman."

Robbie smiled at her wry tone. Unlike her criticism of Hong Kong, that description was right on the nose. Males and females alternating, the figures ranged from skiers and hockey players through runners and tennis players to swimmers in racing suits.

"Nonetheless, it's art of a kind—practical art," Lucretia added. "Not great art, God knows. But even this mishmash takes people out of themselves, shows them something grander. Isn't that what art's supposed to do?"

"Nothing a little more Asian?" he asked. "Not necessarily Buddhist."

"I suppose you know all about Asian art," she said hesitantly, "as well as construction."

"I'd look a chump if I didn't know about Buddhist art," he replied. "I'm meant to be a practicing Buddhist. Not just born to it, not just because my father was. . . . I *chose* Buddhism."

They wound through broad-leafed rhododendrons to a plaza paved with terra-cotta blocks. She pointed with proprietorial pride to the white marble copy of Michelangelo's David at the near end of the plaza. At the far end, a heavy-antlered Chinese dragon was emerging from a slab of granite.

"Some of the ladies objected to David's . . . ah . . . total frontal display." She laughed. "But the dragon, is he Asian enough for you?"

"A beginning. But isn't this all a little hackneyed?"

"I just can't please you today." Her voice rose deprecatingly, as if to apologize. "Can I?"

"That's not so!" he declared. "Really it's all rather like Hong Kong itself, a weird mixture of Occident and Orient."

"Let's see the paintings, then. Afterward, you can take me to lunch . . . if you want to!"

"Nothing in the world I'd rather do." Robbie was happy to prolong the encounter he should have avoided. "I know just the place."

The broad green-marble lobby was, Lucretia pointed out,

mercifully free of the armor and the Scottish broadswords the developers had wanted to hang on the walls. Instead, two large paintings flanked an ornamental rose-marble fireplace. The oil painting on the left was Western in technique, though its subject was traditional China. A woman in the plain white garments of mourning stood before a jagged stone mountain, her hair hanging loose around her shoulders. Her dejected posture, head dropping and shoulders bowed, spoke of sorrow and resignation.

"The wicked concubine Yang Gueifei of the Tang Dynasty just before she was executed by mutinous troops. . . . Her emperor was forced to look on helpless." Robbie was pleased to be on his own ground. "They'd like that, the rich Chinese who live here."

On the right of the fireplace hung an eight-foot-high painting of a city on a cliff overlooking a river. Big bold black and white strokes just touched by color, the technique was neither wholly Western nor wholly Chinese. The painter had created his own form.

"By Wu Guanjong," Lucretia said softly. "*View of Chongqing*. The developers say it cost a hundred fifty thousand."

"Hong Kong dollars, of course," Robbie ventured.

"No, U.S. dollars," she replied. "More than a million Hong Kong."

"Then I won't put in my bid today. Spectacular, isn't it?"

Robbie wandered around the great hall, peering at pictures lit by miniature spotlights in the ceiling. None held him until he came to a landscape that might have been a van Gogh by its bold colors, except that the brushstrokes were too fine and too painstaking. A brilliant field of yellow sunflowers stretched out toward hazy hills in a spare landscape. But an immense black thunderhead hung in the gray-green sky. He leaned forward to read the title: *Storm in Summer: Umbria*, L. Hatton.

"This one's splendid!" he said. "I can smell the dust and the heat and the foreboding in the heavy air."

After a few seconds Lucretia said in a small voice, "I guess that's mine. Hatton was my . . . maiden name. I'm divorced, you know."

"Yes, I've heard. Whatever, the painting's splendid! The best thing here, aside from Wu Guanjong's *Chongqing*. But he works on a different scale. Congratulations, Lucretia. If you can paint like that . . ."

"Have I convinced you?" Delighted by his enthusiasm—and also embarrassed—she turned the talk away from herself. "Don't you see now how worthwhile it is to temper these skyscrapers— these modern cathedrals to the almighty dollar—with human-scale works? Are you persuaded?"

"Pictures and statuary do soften your steel, marble, and glass jungle," he conceded. "I could say I'm all for your idea—just to please you. But it wouldn't be true. My job, among other things, is to keep costs down. I'd have to veto any client who wanted to prettify his building."

"What about all the mirrors in Hong Kong and Beijing . . . all the towers mirrored? Aren't they the same thing? Only pretti-fication, as you'd say?"

"By no means! Mirrors are practical. It's the ricochet effect. Mirrors turn aside evil spirits who want to steal your money or make you ill."

Lucretia scanned Robbie's face. Was he joking slyly, putting her on? Could he really believe this nonsense about evil spirits and demons? She turned away, unable to read his true feelings.

Besides, she was annoyed at him. He'd agreed with her, although with reservations. Then, he had told her he would do nothing to help her. He was very irritating—not least for his unyielding honesty!

Nonetheless, she nodded when he asked, "And now, Miss Hatton, shall we go to lunch?"

3

CONFUSED THOUGHTS CASCADED through Lucretia's mind while she and Robbie waited in front of the white-painted Country Club for the red bus from Shouson Hill to Repulse Bay. Since the explosive chatter of a dozen other waiting passengers made conversation with Robbie impossible, it was a time for reflection.

Her emotions were tumbling over each other. One moment she was serenely content; the next she was exhilarated, yet bewildered. Irked by Robbie's turning down her crusade, she was, nonetheless, happy to be with him.

For the first time since Hong Kong began to wreck her marriage three years earlier, she felt simply wonderful. She also felt protected and secure, as she had not since she was very small. She vividly recalled driving home from Great-Uncle Edward Hatton's in the country when she was only five. The headlights of her father's old Chevrolet had bored a bright yellow tunnel through the black night, and she had drowsed on the backseat, blissfully snug and wholly safe.

The next instant, she felt rash and fearful, as if she were standing at the top of the steepest ski run at Stowe, poised for the dangerous descent. Her stomach clenched at the undercurrent of antagonism that had surfaced during her clashes with Robbie. She had thought him above the nearly universal greed of the Colony, but he had brushed her off by pleading business responsibilities.

And now what? she wondered as the bus approached.

Though frightened, she would not draw back. She glumly told herself that she was not ready for a new commitment so soon after the divorce. Not to Robbie, not to any man—certainly not to Hong Kong itself! Not just yet!

Yet she was strongly drawn to Robbie. Damn him! Why couldn't he at least pretend he was converted to her belief in art in architecture? Why wouldn't he lie to her?

He was taking her to lunch at the Lifeguard Club on Repulse Bay Beach, where not a grain of sand would be seen for the outstretched bodies of fugitives from the stupefying heat of the city. He had wanted to call a taxi. But she had insisted that they wait for the bus, as he would have had he been alone.

They squeezed into the mass of sweating humanity, whose din again made talking impossible. They could not see out windows blocked by the other standing passengers. The overloaded bus careened down the curves of seaside Deep Water Bay Road between the nine-hole golf course and the rows of yachts moored off Middle Island. Flushed with the heat and crushed in the crowd, Lucretia thought wistfully of the air-conditioned Mercedes and Rolls-Royce that had been her normal transport not so long ago. Still, she was glad to be learning through direct experience about the texture of Robbie's daily life.

Robbie himself was secretly relieved. He'd wanted to take a taxi for the privacy it offered, just as he'd chosen the Lifeguard Club for its seclusion. No one who mattered would be riding the jammed bus and see him with her. Nor was the Lifeguard Club frequented at lunchtime by the wealthy and powerful supporters of the impending Communist regime. He knew he should not be seen with Lucretia. But he would for the moment not worry about compromising himself with Beijing. The danger was real, but he would think about it later.

When they got off at Repulse Bay and could talk again, Robbie grimaced and said, "I'm sorry we couldn't see a landmark of my youth, the gray stone castle of the Yu family. Soothsayers warned the Yus that catastrophe would strike if they stopped building. For decades they kept adding bits and pieces to the castle."

"Are they still at it?"

"No!" Robbie smiled wickedly. "They sold out to a developer. That big block of flats just before the beach, that's where the castle stood."

"And catastrophe, did it strike?"

"No and yes. The Yus are richer than ever today. But they did get caught in the battle for Repulse Bay when the Japanese invaded. And after a stock market crash the stockbroker Fisher Yu jumped out of a skyscraper window."

Lucretia liked his deadpan joking, even when it verged on gallows humor. Though he did not gloat over others' misfortunes, his wry observations illuminated their plight—and the human predicament. Besides, he spoke of injustice with indignation.

They passed the Repulse Bay Hotel, a long, low, old-fashioned, yellow-painted stone structure with colonnaded arches overlooking the bay. It now stood before a skyline crammed with high-rise apartments. No more than the terrace dining room of the old hotel had been preserved when the rest was razed to make way for a new hotel.

Having dined there several times, Lucretia now saw it through Robbie's eyes. In the 1930s it had been almost the only building on Repulse Bay. Then war came in 1941. She could all but see and hear the defeated British and Canadian soldiers bowling billiard balls down the teak-planked corridors while awaiting the final Japanese attack.

"Look at that!" Robbie gestured broadly. "Once a glorious old-world hotel with enormous bedrooms, enormous tradition, and enormous panache. Some room-boys and waiters in their seventies had been there all their lives—through the Japanese conquest, through the lean years and the boom years that began in the nineteen-sixties. But now it's only a gimmick, a false facade for another tall square hotel crammed with tiny bedrooms and staffed by Filipinos. It's another Disneyland, phony and cheap! Very soon we'll all be Disney people, homogenized, shiny, and fake friendly. . . . We'll all be totally Americanized!"

Lucretia held her tongue. After all, he wasn't very far from right. Still, she resented his attitude. Was he talking about the vandalized hotel or about herself and the undercurrent of antagonism between them?

"You don't mean Americanized," she said. "The right word is industrialized or computerized, maybe televised, which means hypnotized. It's not America's fault that it leads the world in modern development. . . . Anyway, you have to live in the world and the time you're born into."

He looked hard at her for an instant and veered away from the topic. "Of course, I've only heard about those times, the war and the surrender. But I remember the old hotel—vividly. Mother thought it was wonderful, a touch of the Edwardian glamour her grandparents had known. Once in a blue moon an old friend would ask her to tea there, and she'd be thrilled. . . . We couldn't go near it on our own. How could a genteel, skint widow patronize the Repulse Bay Hotel? We were lucky if we could afford orange squash from the stalls on the beach."

Lucretia did not speak. When Robbie was ready, he would tell her all about his youth and his family. They had plenty of time. Or did they?

Once through the doors of the Lifeguard Club, they were overwhelmed by the noisy greeting of two waiters in white shirts and black trousers. Their uninhibited enthusiasm smacked more of a welcome to an old friend, an equal, rather than deference to a patron. They shook Robbie's hand violently and slapped him on the back, shouting raucous Cantonese insults and laughing uproariously at his replies.

"I was at school with those rascals when I was very small," Robbie explained, and Lucretia filed away another snippet of information about his life. "Before Mother switched me to English-language schools."

When she'd first seen the gaudy facade of the Lifeguard Club from a yacht anchored in Repulse Bay, Lucretia had rather vaguely concluded it was the temple of some outlandish Chinese cult. Thirty-foot-high concrete statues of demigods wearing gorgeous scarlet and blue robes rose above red-tiled peaked roofs. On the broad stairs leading to the beach she had seen statues of animals. Robbie told her the gold Chinese writing on their bases read, "The Heavenly Lion," "The Heavenly Horse," and "The Heavenly Camel."

"Only Cantonese superstition, but touching." He smiled. "For sheer cheek you can't beat the Cantonese of Hong Kong. The giant characters on the stairs say, 'The chief bay in all the world!'"

Ordering was, as always, a lengthy business. A Hong Kong gourmet took as long as a French gourmet choosing food and wine. Robbie was finally satisfied with the menu: minced pigeon with water chestnuts, all to be wrapped in lettuce leaves; scallops sautéed with miniature broccoli and bamboo shoots; conch steamed with a bouquet of spices; and to finish, crisp noodles garnished with scarlet shrimp and tiny violet-tinged squid.

"I hope you're very hungry," Lucretia said. "This isn't lunch, it's a banquet. It'll cost you a fortune."

"Not to worry. My old chums'll see the bill's not too high. And Jacobus will eat anything that's left over."

"Jacobus? One of your waiter pals?"

"Not quite! Jacobus is a shih-tzu, a Tibetan lion dog of great dignity. You must meet him soon."

Pleased at Robbie's hinting that he intended to see her again, Lucretia said, "He sounds enormous and very fierce—a lion dog. Why no Tibetan name?"

"He's called Lishi in Tibetan, the color of gold. He's not large or fierce, only small and feisty and very hairy. He tears a strip off me every evening when I get home, swears at me for leaving him alone. But, somehow, I don't see Jacobus visiting a construction site with me. He's too beautiful. Look, here's a picture."

Jacobus's black face and black beard were all but hidden by a cascade of golden hair. Only his jaunty tail, curved into a circle over his hindquarters, unmistakably distinguished one end of him from the other.

The shih-tzu, that small homey touch, warmed Lucretia's heart, through she wondered why Robbie carried only two photographs in his scuffed wallet. The other, he told her, was his mother, but his set expression warned her not to ask any more questions. He would talk about his mother when he was ready.

Only two photos! Was he so much alone?

"Anyway," she said, "I'd be delighted to meet your little hound . . ."

"Terrier," he corrected. "Terrier and animated burglar alarm. Also a spirited conversationalist and a fine judge of character. You'll see."

Lucretia liked that touch of whimsy: light and amusing, half earnest and half jest, but neither arch nor, the Lord forbid, cute.

"You'll see," he'd said, telling her plainly that this would not be their last time together, not as far as he was concerned. And as far as she was concerned?

The decision to leave Hong Kong or to stay was now pressing. Suppose she told him flatly that she was leaving? Did he care enough to assume the responsibility of asking her to stay? Yet he must not feel she was hustling him, as she was certainly not.

And, if she did stay, how would she live? Her savings would all be gone after a few months, her valuables all sold.

Before meeting Robbie just three days ago she had been poised to leave, yet strangely reluctant to do so. That same evening, she had firmly decided to stay. Yet bored stiff—overwhelmingly, paralytically bored, above all with herself. Her emotions frozen, her hand stayed by apathy, she could not paint. She had also been repelled by her work at the Chinese University. Why should she labor to instill in a new generation of soulless Hong Kong architects an appreciation of beauty?

A Hong Kong architect only had to draw plans for bigger and more angular boxes in which to stow people and desks. Also, perhaps, the occasional gingerbread villa or skyscraper to flaunt its owner's wealth.

How little the Colony had changed, Lucretia reflected, since 1949 when the Communists took China and 1996 when the Communists were preparing to take Hong Kong. Hardly a trace was left of the smug provincial town that had a few decades earlier been the Central District.

She had found photographs dating back to the forties and the fifties on the stands of Hollywood Road beside sepia photographs of naked, shamefaced Chinese women that had even earlier advertised brothels. Half a century ago, low white structures unchanged since the late nineteenth century extended colonnaded canopies over the sidewalks to provide shelter from the searing sun or the pelting rain. Their arches were screened by great roller shades of split bamboo called chicks.

Stick-thin coolies trotted before rickshaws, while other coolies toted monstrous loads on thick bamboo shoulder poles. Corded muscles and purple varicose veins stood out beneath the coolies' sun-blackened skin.

Air conditioning now made massive sunshades unnecessary, and most loads were carried by big wooden-sided trucks or frisky little vans. But a few coolies still trudged under great loads, their plaintive hoots warning pedestrians to clear the way. Their bare-ribbed torsos slick with sweat, some pushed heavily laden carts with screeching wheels, awkwardly dodging Mercedes and Jaguars. Now as then, opium was their chief solace, although Hong Kong had long since banned the black narcotic paste once so profitably smuggled into China.

Lucretia realized that she was fascinated by this metropolis of so many contradictions. A lifetime would not be enough to poke into all its corners and to understand all its ramifications and its nuances. Surely she could devote a few months of her own life to exploring its secrets—under the guidance of Dorje Rabnet.

She would now return to her work enlivened. She would go back to teaching future architects how to draw. She would also strive to reinforce their youthful idealism so that it would endure. When they were practicing architects, perhaps some would abandon the arid clichés of Hong Kong's architecture.

Her thoughts returned to the lion dog, and she said, "Maybe Jacobus would like to know a little more about me. Since he's so finicky about character."

Robbie replied lightly, "His master would, too."

Why not, Lucretia reflected, tell him about herself? She was not a coy teenager in the throes of her first crush, but a mature woman of thirty-two. She would be as candid as he was—or almost as candid.

"I had a conventional happy childhood in Cambridge, Mass," she said. "Sledding and ice-skating, dancing classes, trick or treat at Halloween, turkey and all the works for Thanksgiving and Christmas, fireworks on the Fourth of July. You get the idea. A dog of my own, of course, a setter bitch called Gypsy. She was a darling fool. . . . Mother even baked cookies when she wasn't out doing good works.

"We were all very high-minded, but we certainly didn't live high. Father had a doctorate in linguistics, but he taught English at high school. He said there was less hypocrisy in students or teachers than at a university. So he wasn't paid a fortune. The Hatton family money had all gone with his parents' generation. 'Vanished in dissipation, vanished on slow horses and fast women, on falling stocks and rising expectations,' Father used to say. All we had left, he'd tell us, was high ideals—and a taste for pleasures we couldn't afford.

"We weren't poor, you understand, just—"

The torrent of words stopped abruptly, as if dammed. Despite the air conditioning, Lucretia was flushed and perspiring.

"Why am I telling you all this?" she asked. "Why am I boring you with the unremarkable details of my unremarkable life? And after only one little beer?"

"You're telling me because you want to," he replied evenly. "And nothing you said could ever bore me, especially about yourself. The subject's fascinating. I'm flattered that you want to tell me."

She knew from his even tone that he was not flattering her, and she felt a thrill at his words. He must, she mused, be incapable of insincerity. That damned honesty of his!

"It was cheaper to live at home," she resumed, "so I went to

Radcliffe, right in the middle of Cambridge. Radcliffe when it was still a girls' college, before it was swallowed by Harvard, which devours everything. I got a good degree—Honors plus Phi Beta Kappa. And I set out to paint beautiful pictures. I was just about supporting myself by painting and, of course, by giving art lessons. And I was thinking seriously of going to Italy for a year or two to see where it all began. Then I met Lawrence bloody Barnes and . . ."

Lucretia fell silent a moment, remembering how it was before she'd met Lawrence. She'd been independent. *Dulee* was the Mandarin word for independence, she recalled from her fitful study of that language. Literally, it meant "stand alone." And she had stood alone. Then she had met Lawrence, and then she had left him, and then she was too much alone—cold and lonely.

Robbie smiled, but said nothing. Still, she felt warmed and protected. Perhaps that was what she wanted—no more than to feel safe with this man who seemed to truly care for her.

"I met Lawrence Barnes one rainy day," she went on. "He was in Cambridge for an international lawyers' conference. I met him and fell very hard for his elegance and his phony charm. He appeared sophisticated and polished beside the seedy scholars and self-important professors I was used to. Also, his delightful accent and his English bad manners, his blunt air, seemed to be no more than avoiding hypocrisy. I've learned since that bad manners— especially toward women—are good manners in England. Your typical English gentleman is totally self-indulgent—concentrated entirely on his own pleasure. But this English gentleman was fantastically appealing to an American.

"So I married him, and we came to Hong Kong. And I was

miserable after the first six months or so, when I began to see clearly what I'd gotten myself into.

"An English gentleman in the colonies is *expected* to bully his wife—in public and in private. He's expected to deride and to mock everything she does or wants to do. He's also expected to value her solely as an ornament and a willing handmaiden.

"Lawrence didn't even care particularly what I did with my life—or my body—as long as I was there when he needed me, needed to show off his beautiful wife and her fabulous jewelry and her gorgeous silks and sables. Also, just as long as I didn't make scenes about his little dance-hall girls. I couldn't retaliate in kind. My damnable New England virtue just wouldn't let me take a lover—even if I'd wanted to!"

Lucretia was talking to herself, as well as to Robbie, redefining her own experience.

"You know, he's senior partner of Pope, Mellon, and French. A very British law firm, though most of its business nowadays is with Americans and the Beijing Chinese. He acts for land speculators and builders, also for joint ventures, foreign and Chinese enterprises in China.

"Lawrence swims in a sea of Chinese corruption. The more putrid it gets, the more he prospers. Just like Hong Kong today. And how the money rolls in! The firm pays for the duplex on the Peak. Good Lord, it costs twenty-five, no, thirty thousand US every month. But he's not happy, never has been, despite all that opulence.

"Lawrence is bored with his work. It's too easy to keep the money flowing in. So he drinks like a fish, and he's on and off Prozac. He's a very bright depressive. Also a very serious drinker who regularly makes horrible scenes in public.

"I was bored, too, and I was drinking a bit too much. I was also spending too much money, even though I didn't want to, got no kick out of it. I was frittering away my time listening to too much social chatter. I might have been living in the last days of the Roman empire. Nero and Caligula had nothing on Lawrence's pals and clients. Except his lot doesn't go in for public slaughter of innocents.

"They leave it to Beijing and native capitalists to slaughter for profit in China: factory fires that kill hundreds, mines collapsing, poisoning from toxic waste, more industrial accidents than anywhere else on earth. Of course, no safety regulations are enforced, no more than social security is provided for workers. Also sweatshop pay: casual construction workers get hardly more than a handful of rice. Child labor, practically toddlers, is exploited everywhere: And so on and on and on. . . . Anyway, here we are!"

"What a tale!" Robbie was visibly moved by her account. "It's been damned rough for you, hasn't it? I wish I could make it up to you somehow."

"Just be yourself, Robbie, that's all."

"You know, you're too hard on yourself, Lucretia, too much the New England Puritan. Also, by the way, too hard on Hong Kong. You're right about the super-rich and their hangers-on, a rotten lot. But you misjudge the Colony as a whole. Just hang on while I show you the other side: *my* Hong Kong."

Lucretia felt greatly relieved at having revealed all—or almost all—to Robbie. Since he was sympathetic, not censorious, she was emboldened to make a clean breast of it and added, "I suppose you know I'm working for Martin Lee's Democratic Party?"

Robbie nodded, but his expression was masklike, quite un-readable. Anyway, she hadn't exactly expected him to be pleased at her associating with the Communists' worst enemies.

"Of course, everybody knows everything about everybody else's business in this Colony. . . . Why the Democrats? Because they're working to strengthen our fledgling democracy so the Communists won't be able to stamp it out entirely. I suggest ideas for speeches, design posters, anything else I can do."

"What do you want for *yourself* now?" he asked softly.

"What now?" she mused. "A baby, I suppose. I'm almost thirty-three, and time is running out for me. Yes, I'd like a baby . . . very much so. Also a little security and a little love. Is that too much to ask?" The next moment she wondered if she should have offered that last confession. Had she been too direct? She certainly did not want to frighten him off. She'd already told him so much while he listened so receptively. Now she wanted to tell him everything. If not everything, then as much as a woman ever tells a man.

LUCRETIA AND ROBBIE had for a time been the only patrons in the Lifeguard Club. But others had trickled in, notably a thin Japanese with a fat, nervous Cantonese host hovering over him, and two middle-aged Chinese women who defied the heat of the day with stockings, shawls, and heavy makeup that was beginning to run. But that was all. The business lunch crowd wouldn't venture so far from its offices in Central or Wanchai.

Then a party of five British tourists appeared, three men and two women, all in their thirties. They gossiped in penetrating tones about their friends and commented on their fellow patrons as if no one else could possibly understand English. Each demanded a menu from the waiter, and each ordered individually, as if in a Berni's Steak House. The waiters shook with silent laughter when they placed before each member of the party a platter of sweet and sour pork. Hardly a house specialty for a seafood restaurant, that was the ultimate cliché for foreigners in any Chinese restaurant. Each of the tourists solemnly picked up his chopsticks and clumsily attacked his own dish. No one had told them that the essential charm of Chinese cuisine was the variety of sharing different dishes.

Robbie's former schoolmates, the waiters, had preserved his privacy. No one else was seated near their window overlooking the bay. Across heat-hazed waters they could just make out vague shapes that were distant islands. Intent on each other, they had ignored the view until they ended their meal with fresh papaya and were sipping astringent tea. While Robbie stared across the water, Lucretia studied the tea leaves in her handleless cup.

Finding no satisfaction there, she glanced up and followed his gaze. A few Chinese junks and Western sloops were just appearing on the horizon. On that Friday afternoon, the toilers of the sea would be preparing their lanterns, their tridents, and their nets for the evening's fishing. For the privileged it was the beginning of a long weekend of pleasure. From adjoining moorings the work-bound and the pleasure-bound were setting out across waters littered with orange peel, rubber flip-flops, cardboard cartons, plastic bags, and even less salubrious waste.

The big white motor yachts that real sailors called gin palaces were already moving in stately procession past Repulse Bay toward the Stanley Peninsula and the Po Toi Islands, where the water was somewhat less polluted. The boat-boys would drop anchor and lower the swimming ladders. While owners and guests took a few turns around the bulbous hulls, the boat-boys would lay out lavish food and abundant drink. The privileged, many now Hong Kong and Beijing Chinese, as well as foreigners, would then devote themselves to the serious business of eating and drinking.

Nowadays, less drink was consumed and more food, particularly by the Chinese. Almost passed was the heroic drinking of the early days of the century, when an anchorage in New Territories had been called—with literal accuracy—Gin Drinkers' Bay.

The pretext for that mighty consumption had been the belief the gin kept the mosquitoes away because they hated the smell! Nowadays potent sprays kept insect pests down. Eradicated decades earlier by stringent destruction of breeding places, mosquitoes were now coming back, all but invited by both official and private laxness as the handover drew close.

A covey of white-sailed boats scattered from their anchorage at Middle Island. In the vanguard were three long narrow craft Lucretia recognized as dragons, an old once popular design. Behind them came a half dozen bigger sailing craft with sleek deckhouses. In the rear, a dozen or so small sailing dinghies began to race around the orange buoys bobbing in Repulse Bay.

Their triangular white sails danced like drifting snow on green wavelets. The varied flags at their sterns streamed in the breeze as if in an international regatta, kind of a water carnival: yellow and blue; green, red, and white; red, white, and blue.

Hard on the wakes of the pleasure craft came the working craft: first small sampans trailing fine white nets, many sculled by long stern-oars in the hands of lean, black-trousered figures under mushroom-shaped bamboo hats.

Bigger sampans propelled by outboard motors were straddled by pairs of powerful lights. When dusk fell, their brilliant rays would attract fish and squid to be skewered by spearlike tridents. The long shining arc those craft made against the dark sky would heighten the illusion of a blithe water carnival.

Against the backdrop of the big container ships and the great tankers steaming through the narrow channel between Lamma Island and Hong Kong Island there came the big working craft. Teak-planked junks shaped like great slippers a hundred feet long pounded over the waves under diesel power. Their remnant masts, no longer flaunting sails, supported twisted webs of nets that would trail for thousands of yards through the deeper water farther offshore. Two junks meandered in the opposite direction, moved by fragile-looking tea-brown sails spread like vast fans on bamboo ribs.

"Quite a sight!" Robbie grinned at Lucretia. "The whole fleet's a stirring sight, isn't it? You're lucky to see big working junks under sail. Hong Kong uses a sailing junk symbol to lure tourists. But the only ones actually under sail now are Chinese."

"You can't have everything." She smiled. "But how could I ever paint it—and not make it a cliché? I don't know—"

"It can't be, can't possibly!" he broke in, then spoke a few words in Cantonese to the waiter.

"I don't believe what I'm seeing. . . ." Robbie took a pair of large naval binoculars from the waiter and adjusted them. He studied whatever it was that had so astonished him before silently handling the binoculars to Lucretia. His pointing index finger showed her where to look.

"By God, it must be," he said softly. "What do you see?"

"Something big and shiny behind a longish boat. It's not a barge, more a sort of bubble. Yes, I can see it now. The black boat's towing the bubble—at high speed to judge from the rooster tail wake. Now that is something different!"

"And inside the bubble?" he asked. "What can you make out?"

"Nothing yet. . . . Yes, I see it now. Something big and black. . . . No, it can't be! The black thing's a car. A big one . . . a Mercedes, I think."

"Full marks," he said. "I thought I was dreaming."

"This is weird, Robbie. What's it all about?"

"Theft . . . grand larceny. Somebody in Canton, some powerful official or some new rich entrepreneur, ordered the car stolen, probably the very car that has taken his fancy. Most convenient delivery of a stolen car is in an enormous great plastic bag towed up the Pearl River. The People's Police are well bribed to turn a blind eye. The People's Navy's also in the racket up to their necks. It's a great trick for a dark night—grab the car, drive down to the shore at a little-used spot—and, presto, into the bubble."

He grinned at her wide-eyed astonishment at the extraordinary sight. It was hard to believe this brazen daylight robbery was actually occurring.

"It looks like the Hong Kong police are well into the racket," he observed. "Turning a blind eye at night's easy. But by day! Somebody's been well greased to let the gang operate in daylight. More convenient, less danger of hitting something. Well, I'll be damned!"

Lucretia had recovered from her surprise, for she believed there was no limit to Hong Kong chicanery. Nonetheless, it was phenomenal, the enormous, air-buoyant plastic bag skipping over the wavelets.

"Like a magic bubble!" she said and smiled at her own fantasy. "If we could only slip into a magic bubble, just the two of us, and be carried far away."

4

TWO WEEKS HAD passed since Lucretia and Robbie's first encounter at the photographer's shop on the Peak. Since then they had met nearly every day, kept apart only by her teaching schedule or his trip to a distant construction site. The mutual understanding so quickly formed was almost beyond the need for words.

But not quite. Lucretia was intensely aware that barriers they could not yet surmount separated them. Robbie, too, had reservations. Though he, no more than she, wished to talk about those barriers, neither their minds nor their bodies could yet attain complete intimacy.

To celebrate their second full week since they'd met Robbie took Lucretia to the Luk Yu Teahouse on a steep street above Queen's Road Central. Luk Yu was China's legendary God of Tea. He had discovered the bushes from whose leaves he, first of all mortals, infused a heavenly beverage.

Itself discovered a decade earlier by tourist guides, the Luk Yu could have been swamped by outsiders and become another fake Chinesey tourist trap. Fortunately, its charm was too slight and its ambience too restrained to attract many outsiders.

Old men wearing Chinese long gowns still came to sip tea, to smoke pinches of tobacco in the tiny metal bowls of their long-stemmed pipes, and to gossip. Many brought their pet birds to take the air and to see new sights. The birds' lacquered bamboo cages hung from hooks set in the wall between showpieces of Chinese calligraphy brushed in black ink.

The distinct fragrances of a hundred varieties of tea mingled with the scent of the chrysanthemum, rose, and jasmine petals that flavored some varieties. Those subtle, delicate scents were complemented by the robust aromas of the steamed or fried tidbits called dim sum and the strong smells of soya sauce and vinegar. The atmosphere happily combined the refinement of classic Chinese culture with the hearty enjoyment of earthy pleasures that was also typically Chinese.

"The Luk Yu's a vestige," Robbie said. "It's like Hong Kong was decades ago. But teahouses are coming back all over China. And there's a Sunday market in Beijing that sells only living things: tropical fish and pet birds. It's all very Buddhist—not Communist at all."

Lucretia did not probe, although she was anxious to learn more about his Buddhist faith. She was sometimes tantalized by his reticence, sometimes just annoyed. But she counseled herself to wait until he revealed both his faith and his deepest feelings in his own time.

Their waiter brought a fine-pored earthenware teapot. On its rotund terra-cotta bowl sinuous Chinese characters traced an enigmatic message.

"Savor this splendid tea calmly!" Robbie translated and added, "Sip it very slowly. It's *loongjing,* dragon well, one of the most precious of the great teas of China."

Sometimes, Lucretia decided, Robbie was a shade too instructive. He was gradually showing her "the real Hong Kong," which was radically different from slick restaurants like the Trattoria, Gaddi's, and Joyce's or luxury hotels like the Mandarin and the Regent. She knew those playpens of the rich well, but not the reality of the community in which they were set. He was introducing her to the other side of the Colony, whose values were strange to her, its behavior often alien. Not surprisingly, he sometimes overdid it. But she had already learned that the working people of Hong Kong shared common aspirations and a common decency with working men and women elsewhere—as the cynical and profligate new rich did not.

As instructed, she sipped the pale gold liquid in the small porcelain cup. The flavor was allusive, too subtle, perhaps, for an untrained palate, let alone an untrained foreign palate.

But Robbie's real Hong Kong was by and large anything but subtle. His Colony was brash, coarse, greedy, insensitive—and bursting with vitality. It was also violent, sometimes murderous, though reasonably impartial British law had for more than a century been evenhandedly enforced by the Royal Hong Kong Police.

In the past the people of Hong Kong had grudgingly respected their government. Most were, however, now furious with the British—not for high-handed colonial rule, but for withdrawing abjectly. The police were prudently dropping the title "Royal," which they had won by suppressing a virtual Communist insurgency three decades earlier. Rather comically, traditional red postboxes had been replaced because they displayed the royal crown.

Such crawling had engendered scorn for the outgoing British administration, despite the courageous stand of the last British governor. Since the public were now contemptuous of British law and the British-trained police, serious crime was increasing throughout the small territory. The hijacked Mercedes in the plastic bubble was only one symptom of that pestilence.

"The British want more trade with China, the world's fastest-growing economy," Lucretia had often heard it said, and further: "So they're giving Hong Kong to Beijing on a golden platter. Maybe the biggest bribe ever offered anyone anywhere: more than $US60 billion in cash, plus public buildings, docks, airports, and tunnels worth hundreds of billions more."

The public's apprehension mirrored Lucretia's personal misgivings. She nonetheless lifted her cup to Robbie and said, "A toast to us! Whether what we have found lasts or withers, to us!"

"I'll drink to that!" he responded. "Though of course it'll last!"

Lucretia wondered how much he understood her roiled feelings. Perhaps, she mused, it was better that he did not completely understand.

Self-esteem lacerated by her disastrous marriage, she now shied from any new commitment. She was, quite simply, afraid. She dared not give her trust or her affection wholly, for she knew she was now incapable of sustaining a lasting relationship.

No logic backed her judgment, only shrill instinct and irrational emotion. She all but panicked when she envisioned giving herself to Robbie unreservedly. Her stomach clenched, and her breathing grew ragged as her body implored her to remain safe by rejecting obligation.

Although she would bring those physical reactions under control, she was also deterred by practical considerations. She was by no means sure she wanted to live in Hong Kong at all, much less live in Hong Kong under Beijing's rule as the wife of a man whose career would always be handicapped by his mixed blood. And if, as she ardently wished, there were children, what would they become?

"I'll grant you," he said, refilling their cups, "that some good practical reasons look like being against us."

Having decided to let Robbie set the pace, Lucretia did not question him. He had already told her he was no longer deterred by fear that his work would suffer from his associating with her. Too strongly attracted to heed that peril, he now swore again: The devil with playing it safe!

That impulsive decision was to Lucretia the true measure of his love. He had been drilled to prudence. His profession required him to double-check every specification, and, if in doubt, to triple-check. Many lives and much valuable property could be lost if he did not get his calculations absolutely right. His professional caution had seeped into his very nature. In his personal life, too, he rarely made an impulsive gesture.

"You're funny sometimes, Robbie," she mused aloud. "Funny peculiar, not funny ha ha. So cautious! I bet this is the first time you've ever made up your mind so fast. About me, I mean. But not about the future."

She did not, of course, know that he was still pondering the brides pressed upon him by the Colony's small Tibetan community and by his father's family in Lhasa. His grandmother had not even told him who the woman was, but only that he must marry her soon. Prudently, he had not yet decided whether he would marry either—or neither.

"Look here," he began tentatively. "I've learned something, too. I'm not immune to overpowering emotion. I've got an impulsive streak, no question about it."

Nor did he confess that he was all but ready to cast all others aside for this bewitching American woman whom he had known so briefly. Yet after the first raptures of discovering each other, they would have to live with others in the real world. It might well be easier for Lucretia to live in Beijing's new Special Administrative Region than for himself.

Despite her divorce, despite her repudiation of her former husband's world, despite her erroneous reputation as a right-wing radical, Lucretia was still welcome in the circles where major decisions were made. It was, Robbie judged, a matter of habit—and also a matter of race.

The nominal rulers under the outgoing British governor were now largely the Hong Kong Chinese civil servants. The higher echelons mingled with the super-rich, who were now also chiefly Hong Kong Chinese. But a white face was still an asset—particularly the captivating face of a charming woman. Many so-called Europeans, which really meant whites, were still in good standing in those ruling circles.

Money spoke in peremptory tones in the Crown Colony. Money dictated most important decisions, despite a maverick governor and a largely elected legislature who were reaching together toward greater democracy. Money would continue to dictate until July 1, 1997, when the People's Liberation Army marched in.

Quite likely afterward as well, although some powerful men in Beijing wanted Hong Kong to decline—to be replaced as a major financial center by a resurgent Shanghai. Other powerful men in Beijing would, however, strive to protect Hong Kong. They were determined that the territory would continue to enrich them secretly by openly further enriching both the home-grown multimillionaires who had come over to Beijing and the new red multimillionaires who ran the Communists' multi-billion-dollar businesses in the Colony. Whichever faction triumphed, Beijing would always have the last word in Hong Kong.

"Robbie, why is it?" Lucretia interrupted her own train of thought.

"Why is what?" he laughed.

"Why are our lives so mixed up with other people's politics? It's not fair!"

"Whatever else, your Jack Kennedy did say one memorable truth. *Life isn't fair!* So let's make the best of it."

"What does that mean, my friend?"

"It means we should take our pleasure when we can. *All* the pleasures open to two loving minds and bodies—female and male."

They had kissed for the first time only a week earlier—and had then no more than brushed lips. They were too old to cuddle like teenagers, too passionate perhaps to endure the frustration of arousal without consummation. Robbie was eager to seal their great affection with their bodies. Lucretia knew she was falling in love, but was in no great hurry to celebrate that love in bed.

"I knew all along you only wanted to get me into the sack," she laughed. For a moment he looked hurt, but then barked with laughter.

"I was only teasing." She chuckled. "I know you're no Don

Juan! But let's not rush into bed. Let's allow our love to grow slowly, naturally. Then it'll last—if it's truly fated."

Her hesitation stemmed, above all, from their divergent cultures, which might turn out to be antipathetic as well. She was warmed by his admiration and moved by his ardent affection. She had never been wooed with such fierce enthusiasm. She was also aroused by his touch, as she had never been by any other's. Still, if they were too old to paw each other like teenagers, she hoped she was now too wise to commit herself totally to any man on such brief acquaintance.

Particularly not a man who, for all his Anglicized charm, his natural candor, and his unfeigned ardor, had grown up in Hong Kong. He had, naturally, absorbed the small Colony's peculiar values and its bizarre standards of behavior, so alien to her. He was, further, heir to the even more alien culture of Tibet. The Tantric Buddhism he professed sounded to her, at least in part, like rarified mumbo-jumbo. She was still reading with strained attention the tomes on Tibet she had found in the City Hall Library.

LUCRETIA FELT VAGUELY out of sorts when Robbie and she left the Luk Yu and strolled aimlessly toward the amusement quarter called Lan Kwai Fong. Why could she not take her fate in her own hands and make a firm decision as to where her life was going? Lan Kwai Fong always depressed her. Literally Orchid and Flower Market, it was so far removed from overwhelmingly Chinese work-a-day Hong Kong that it made her feel like an interloper in the Colony.

Lan Kwai Fong was tailored to the fantasies of the young foreigners who now swarmed in their tens of thousands through the Colony. Many were engaged in the semimystical trade called financial services, for Hong Kong stood almost on a level with New York, London, and Frankfurt in manipulating money. That craft required more nerve than brains, bold effrontery more than logical deliberation, and, above all, luck. When free of their telephones and their trading screens, those financial servants rambunctiously relieved the tension bred by their long hours, their head-aching concentration, and their weighty responsibilities.

Lan Kwai Fong offered restaurants whose decor, beverages, and cuisine derived, however freely, from all the world: Indochina and Greece, Spain and Australia, New York and Tokyo, India and Portugal. Its chief pursuit was serious drinking in scores of bars. One memorable New Year's Eve some twenty youths had been trampled to death by the carefree throngs.

The foreign women were less abandoned than the men, even those engaged in the same arcane trade. The swarm of Chinese girlfriends in micro-miniskirts and buttock-hugging jeans, who were by and large teetotalers, appeared to be fresh-minted from the same mold every year. So alike were they to each other and to their predecessors they might have been one vast family. They made Lucretia feel ancient, remembering that she was close to thirty-three.

Robbie smiled wryly, but did not speak. He detested Lan Kwai Fong for its phony chic and its counterfeit sophistication. Besides, it was so modern and so utterly foreign, little to do with the essential Crown Colony.

At the beginning of the century a tranquil flower market had occupied the site. Tranquil as far as anything involving the vehement and noisy Cantonese could be tranquil. Regardless, flowers were greatly to be preferred to fake foreign facades and juvenile foreigners' antics.

In the 1950s, when refugees from China arrived in their hundreds of thousands, the quarter had been a warren of low dilapidated buildings that housed food shops, eating houses, gambling parlors, money changers, native banks, and brothels. It had pulsed with real life—real suffering and real joy.

The sharp odors and the little street dramas, both redolent of old Hong Kong and old China, had vanished. No longer was the breeze scented by mold, damp plaster, wood smoke, and the pungent medicine shops that stocked tiger bones, ginseng, and rhinoceros horn, as well as a thousand herbal remedies. Instead, the quarter stank of beer, vomit, french fries, and cheap perfumes.

No longer did passersby see ancient ladies supported by canes or servants totter across cobblestones on tiny bound feet in velvet slippers. No longer did emaciated sedan-chair bearers wait for customers before the offices of *The South China Morning Post*. The *Post* had moved its headquarters miles away, and the chair bearers were all dead, their sedan-chairs broken up for firewood or bought from dubious heirs by small museums. Filipina maids in bright blouses or printed T-shirts worn above miniskirts or tight jeans now strolled where decorous lesbian amahs wearing immaculate white tunics and wide black trousers had once chosen flowers for their masters' households.

Robbie again vented his anger at Lan Kwai Fong's transformation into a playground for young foreigners: "They've turned it into a downmarket Disneyland!"

Lucretia, clinging to Robbie's arm to keep from being swept

away by the jostling crowd, only smiled. This was no time to argue with him.

Robbie was all but obsessed with Disneyland as the epitome of the decadent West. Despite his love for his doughty English mother, he was inclined to characterize as foreign almost everything that was unwholesome, corrupt, false, or loathsome. A psychobabbler might say he was compensating for his own uncomfortable position between two worlds.

Yet for herself Hong Kong proved the good that could come of the joining of East and West. After all, the Crown Colony's amazing prosperity and its concern for the less fortunate were at least as much due to foreigners as to Chinese. Otherwise, why had the Chinese not done as well elsewhere on their own? Otherwise, why did Beijing prate about its love for the people, but not provide even the minimal welfare services Hong Kong did?

Without Britain, she concluded, Hong Kong would not exist. Nor would Shanghai. But that was a sore subject. Anyway, they could hardly hear each other over the pandemonium of cars, trucks, buses, and raucous Cantonese conversation.

The buildings framing the intersection of Queen's Road and Pedder Street were constantly under construction or demolition. But the spirit of that crossroads had remained unaltered for decades, as had the danger of being crushed by the hurrying crowds. Clustered around the old Queen's Cinema, a melange of small stores, stalls, hawkers, fast-food joints, and exuberantly expensive famous-brand-name shops on the level of Celine, Armani, and Tiffany's bewildered tourists and natives alike. Lucretia believed it was the most crowded and tumultuous corner anywhere, making Times Square and Piccadilly Circus seem leisurely backwaters.

"What's that?" she exclaimed.

"Maybe a car backfiring," he replied. "Not to worry."

The low, bass report sounded again—and was abruptly cut off, like resounding cymbals when the bandsman claps them to his chest. Perhaps it was blasting. Constant din was one price of the Colony's frenetic prosperity: not only blasting, but the whine of cranes, the chatter of jackhammers, and the grumbling of bulldozers.

But this was different. Across broad Pedder Street pedestrians were, as usual, bunched before the Landmark, a three-story shopping mall capped by fifty-story towers. That gleaming citadel of glitzy Hong Kong was, as usual, sucking in shoppers and spewing out other shoppers. Strangely, however, the pedestrians were retreating toward Queen's Road.

Forced back by the crowd already cramming Queen's Road, the massed pedestrians bulged into the roadway of Pedder Street, heedless of taxies and minibuses contending with big buses and torrents of private cars. Abruptly that bulge disintegrated into fleeing individuals and couples.

The low-pitched report sounded again—and was immediately followed by high-pitched reports strung so close together Lucretia could not hear the individual explosions. It sounded like a heavy-duty zipper opening so violently it tore the thick fabric in which it was set.

Robbie frowned and muttered, "A revolver and an automatic rifle dueling?"

Lucretia now clung to his arm to keep from being borne away by the panicky crowd. Robbie pushed into the entrance of the Citibank. Surrounded by plate glass that could fragment into razor-edged splinters if struck by a stray bullet, they were hardly better off than they had been in the open.

"Good God!" Robbie exclaimed, and Lucretia craned her neck to see over his shoulder.

A lean policeman sprawled on his back in the middle of Pedder Street. Shaken drivers just managed to wheel around his still figure. An instant later, the cars, vans, and buses had escaped toward the waterfront. No new vehicles took their place. The roadway was empty except for the fallen constable in knife-edge-pressed trousers of tan cotton and a short-sleeved safari jacket. The chrome number on his shoulder straps was backed by red to show that he spoke English. His blue-serge peaked cap tumbled in the light breeze, and his big revolver lay just beyond his splayed fingers.

Another constable crouched behind an abandoned Toyota taxi. Seeing no pedestrians in the line of fire, he edged around the scarlet taxi. His revolver jerked in his hand twice. In the hush that had replaced the normal Hong Kong din, the shots sounded lower and louder. Rather, Robbie thought, like an old lion roaring in rage.

On the corner across the street a reinforced plate-glass window splintered, laying open Tiffany's, the supremely fashionable international jewelers. A shrill cry rose from the shop, and high-pitched staccato bursts of bullets hosed Pedder Street, which now seemed very narrow. Neither the constable nor the unwilling spectators were touched, although the bullets made a colander of the taxi.

"We do get into the damnedest situations, don't we?"

Lucretia's laughter was shaky. But she realized in surprise that she was not really afraid, though she was in danger. It was too much like watching a gangster movie from a comfortable theater seat.

She was acutely aware of the heat generated by the close-pressed crowd when perspiration trickled between her breasts and down her back. She sniffed the normal odors of a Hong Kong summer's day: garlic frying, gasoline fumes, melting road tar, and cigarette smoke—also the stench of sweating bodies.

Robbie was apparently unaware that he was whistling softly his favorite old song about God, little green apples, and Indianapolis. She was pressed hard against him, and that was a great comfort. When the low whistling stopped, she glanced up to see him grinning fiercely. A gene from a hard-fighting Khampa warrior must have triggered his glee. Evidently becoming aware of his bellicose grimace, he assumed a grave expression.

Seven constables wearing tan uniforms and blue-serge caps were now crouched behind abandoned cars and a stalled red bus. They rose momentarily to fire their revolvers at Tiffany's. They were answered by the testy high-pitched ping of assault rifles and the spasmodic clatter of an old submachine gun. The crowd heaved, instinctively trying to shrink into itself like a tortoise into its shell. But the involuntary spectators were jammed too tight to run away—and were, perhaps, also too fascinated.

Siren wailing, a navy-blue van skidded to a halt on the sticky roadway. Twelve policemen poured out and dived for cover. Their tan trousers bloused over gleaming black combat boots, they also wore navy-blue berets and black flak jackets. Though big revolvers in black leather holsters hung from their belts, all carried automatic rifles, shotguns, or machine pistols.

Their first shots drew a high-pitched volley from the unseen gangsters trapped in Tiffany's. A constable with the broad face and the stocky body of a Cantonese peasant looked down stolidly at the red patch that dyed his sleeve below the chrome chevrons of a sergeant. After perhaps twenty seconds, he shook his head in annoyance and abruptly sat down on the pavement.

"Shock!" Robbie said into Lucretia's ear. "Whoever's inside, they're firing Kalashnikovs, AK-47s. A nasty weapon."

Lucretia wondered how he could be so sure. To identify a weapon by its report was, she assumed, no great trick for a trained soldier. But it seemed an odd accomplishment in a peaceful civil engineer.

A gasp from the onlookers punctuated the exchange of fire. A rifle with a banana-curved magazine was extended butt-first from the doorway of Tiffany's; a white cloth spotted by blood fluttered on the barrel to signal surrender. A slight figure in grimy cotton trousers and shirt hurtled from the doorway onto the deserted sidewalk. A police inspector emerged from behind a red bus and beckoned to the gunman, who threw his AK-47 into the roadway.

"*Touxiang! Touxiang!*" he shouted. "*Jiuming!*"

"I surrender!" Robbie's voice murmuring into her ear heightened the scene's grotesque likeness to a Chinese gangster movie dubbed into English. "Spare me!"

Fearing his confederates' revenge, the gunman scrabbled on hands and knees for cover behind an abandoned silver BMW. A single AK-47 rattled from Tiffany's, and a string of small holes stitched themselves across his grimy white back.

His own momentum carried the wounded gunman close to the wounded sergeant. While still moving forward, he stiffened and collapsed to lie unmoving no more than ten feet from the doorway where Robbie and Lucretia huddled among the packed crowd. A true movie climax—the gangster dying at their feet.

Lucretia turned her horrified gaze away from the slight figure with the diagonal stripe of blood crossing his back like the scarlet sash of some macabre order of chivalry. His face, sharply lit by the morning sun, somehow appeared alien to Hong Kong. His features were quite ordinary, but his skin was rough and chapped, its hue pallid, almost ashen. Grime was ingrained across his forehead, and his flat nose bore a sprinkling of blackheads. His patched blue trousers, his cheap sneakers trodden flat at the heel, and his filthy, tattered shirt further showed that he was impoverished. Hardly any Hong Kong man was so dirty or so battered.

The gunman was clearly from the mainland. Lucretia had heard that staff officers at Liberation Army headquarters in Canton lent thugs to the Triads, the Colony's criminal societies. Those mainland gangsters were usually violent, hardly blinking at murder.

Lucretia wondered: another sign of the times?

Enraged at the slaying of their captive, the police poured volleys into the jeweler's. The closest hurled stun grenades, which were nonlethal, technically at least. Yet, feeling the shock waves, Lucretia knew the police were no longer trying to capture the gang, but shooting to kill.

The next instant it was all over. The police fire was no longer returned. After cautiously waiting for three or four minutes, a few policemen gingerly entered the shattered shop. Two white-clad ambulance men followed insouciantly, and two minutes later carried out the first stretcher. A gray blanket covered a still form, but puddled blood dripped through the canvas stretcher.

A constable emerged from Tiffany's dangling three AK-47s by their slings. Clearly incredulous, he gazed at the weapon in his left hand: a green-painted submachine gun with a circular magazine and a perforated shield around the barrel. Such old Chinese weapons appeared in photographs of the Korean War. Lucretia looked away, the fascination the small battle had exerted having vanished.

"When I was young," Robbie said abruptly, "you'd draw two years in quod if the bobbies found you with an old pistol without a firing pin. Now we're knee-deep in assault rifles and submachine guns."

He knuckled his eyes irritably and said, "About time you met Jacobus the lion dog. Will you honor us by visiting our small flat? And who knows what else—"

Robbie's candor was refreshing as well as flattering. He made no bones about wanting to make love to her. She was not yet ready, but he would assuredly wait. Anyway, she'd feel downright foolish if, like a timid Victorian damsel, she refused to venture into a man's apartment.

Clutching her arm possessively, he led her to the shelter where the double-decker trams stopped. He was whistling softly, but not about little green apples, rain, and Indianapolis. She remembered the chorus of the old song about loving someone till the twelfth of never.

5

THE SMALL ELEVATOR blasted upward with the velocity of a ballistic missile. Lucretia's heart was in her throat, her stomach almost in the basement.

"I've told the house committee they've got to pressurize the lift like an airliner." Robbie grimaced. "But so far no joy."

His apartment was on the thirty-fourth floor of one of those gray towers that rose in clumps of six to eight buildings on land reclaimed from the harbor between Wanchai and Causeway Bay.

"How do you find your way home?" Lucretia asked. "The towers are all the same."

"If I go to apartment thirty-four-A in the wrong building, a stranger opens the door," he laughed.

"Bought it ten years ago," he volunteered as the elevator doors popped open. "I had to scrape up the deposit and pay off the remaining two hundred thousand in eight years. Now it's meant to be worth a million, maybe two. But how can I sell it? Got to have somewhere to live."

The steel grill in front of his door was secured by a steel bar and three locks. The door itself was reinforced with a steel plate and secured by four locks.

"An Englishman's home is his castle! Same here. All I need is a moat and a drawbridge." Robbie shrugged in disgust. "Makes you weep, the way we live in Hong Kong. Every last flat's fortified against burglars and Triads."

"At least they don't shoot their way in," she said. "Not like those miserable gunmen today. Poor dupes, they were just thrown into the fire!"

"No, others don't shoot. Not yet! But they will!"

"Beijing's already sent us its violence and its corruption," she observed. "Is worse to come when Beijing takes over?"

Robbie grunted to acknowledge her question. But he did not comment. He was evidently determined to see no evil, to hear no evil, and, above all, to speak no evil about the Communists' impending rule.

While he twirled combinations and turned keys, Lucretia did some quick mental arithmetic. Two hundred thousand Hong Kong dollars, the apartment's original price, was roughly twenty-six thousand US. And Robbie could now sell it for a million and a half Hong Kong, say US two hundred thousand. But he'd have to pay at least that much to buy another apartment that was no better, perhaps worse. Renting was a mug's game, just throwing money away.

The apartment was very basic: bedroom, living/dining room, kitchen, and bath, all minuscule. Also a kitchen window that offered a wonderful view of Kowloon, Robbie said, if you leaned far out and twisted your head hard left. Hardly luxury, the apartment exuded the universal Hong Kong smell of mold and plaster that never quite dried. Lucretia felt confined. Robbie's apartment, what there was of it, bred claustrophobia.

She was, however, cheered by the heavy-antlered dragon sporting on the yellow Tibetan carpet and by the gleaming brass seven-foot-long Tibetan horn hanging on the wall. The small sofa was upholstered in a colorful floral pattern. Despite those cheerful touches, the apartment was hardly more than basic shelter. Behind the sofa, casement windows looked out on the casement windows of another apartment. As if peering from the bottom of a well, she could just see a patch of cloud-flecked sky above.

A small dog stood four-square on the dragon, imperiously demanding attention with *basso profundo* barks worthy of a mastiff. Jacobus the lion dog stood no more than nine inches high.

When she stooped to stroke him, Jacobus met her halfway. His plumed golden tail, normally curled above his back, standing out straight as a flagpole, flailed from side to side. His head bobbed with each bark. When he paused, the tip of his tongue protruded, pale pink in his black face. His large dark eyes gleamed beneath his fringe of golden hair, which was drawn into a flaring topknot secured by a blue elastic band.

Lucretia wanted to pick him up and hug him. She had once heard a buyer for F.A.O. Schwarz on his way to the sweatshops of China say he dealt in "plush animals." Jacobus looked just like a plush animal, impeccably groomed and exceedingly dignified.

"What enthusiasm!" Robbie said. "He's usually wary of strangers. You know, he's a professional watchdog."

"A watchdog?" Lucretia laughed. "What would he do to a burglar, lick him to death?"

"His bark's enough to scare off any burglar. He comes from a long line of temple guardians whose only weapon is their loud barking. It's not what you are that counts, my grandmother says, but what people think you are."

"What's worth stealing in the temples?"

"Only gold and silver vessels, jeweled prayer wheels and boxes, priceless old books, that sort of thing. In the end, the Chinese got almost all . . . stole them. They weren't impressed by loud barking—or by the tears and lamenting of nuns and monks. Then the Chinese got rid of them, too."

Disconcerted by his mild outburst, Robbie stepped into the tiny kitchen, which was only a stride away. Startled by his uncharacteristic fervor, Lucretia watched in silence while he opened the minuscule refrigerator, found a bottle of white wine, and pulled the cork. He filled two wineglasses, set them on the hammered copper coffee table, and sat beside her on the small sofa. She leaned toward him, and his arm encircled her shoulders.

"I know you're good-looking, well-mannered, kindhearted, humorous, and honest." Her light tone was meant to camouflage the electric shock she felt at his touch, but her voice trembled minutely. "And that's all I know. I know nothing about your family, your background. Your grandmother, for one. And Jacobus, why you dote on him. So much I don't know about you."

"Why not ask me some questions?"

"Oh, Robbie, don't be dense." She paused for a moment, suddenly shy. But she had to tell him. "Maybe it's only infatuation. Maybe I love you. I can't say, not so soon. I *do* want you to . . . make love to me. But I know so little about you. I might as well make love with a handsome shop window dummy. You're a man of mystery."

Lucretia leaned closer, tilting her face up. She kissed him long and hard, as if to prove how much she wanted him. Nor did she draw back when his hands strayed over her back and downward. Not she, but he abruptly broke off the embrace and rose from the sofa.

Jacobus had been barking furiously. When Robbie drew away from her, the lion dog fell silent.

"Jacko's a real passion-killer." Robbie chuckled. "He's dead jealous. Only thing'll shut him up's a big meaty shinbone."

Lucretia bit her tongue. She simply would not ask: How do you know that? Do you bring many easy ladies here?

"I'm no mystery," Robbie resumed. "Just an average Hong Kong chap. Does this vertical hovel look like the residence of a man of mystery and power?"

"Anything but," she acknowledged.

"You asked about Jacobus. He's a true Tibetan, born in Lhasa. My grandmother sent him to me—as a sort of talisman."

Robbie studied Lucretia with the wistful eyes of a man in love with a woman who did not know whether she was in love with him. She perched on the arm of the sofa, her posture graceful but tense. A candy-striped T-shirt clung to her breasts, while tight cream-colored linen slacks hugged her hips and her legs. Her hands were clasped around one knee. Bare of lipstick after their kiss, her mouth was taut, and a faint vertical line separated her moth-wing eyebrows.

"For centuries furry dogs like Jacko've lived with Tibetans. Unlike Western religions, Buddhism doesn't set humans totally apart from other animals. Our little lion dogs and our giant mastiffs are all part of a continuum, an unbroken progression to humanity. Mankind may be at the top of the ladder, but the others are all on the same ladder. So Grandmother gave me a shih-tzu puppy, a living part of our history and tradition."

"You grew up in Hong Kong, didn't you? A typical Hong Kong chap, you said a minute ago. How come a Tibetan grew up in Hong Kong?"

"Simple! My mother was here, so I was born here. There've always been a few Tibetans in Hong Kong—traders, teachers, monks, and so forth. More since the Chinese Communists took over our country. Three or four hundred now. We stick together. We have to with Chinese swarming all around us!"

"Your father was a trader?"

"Anything but!" Robbie laughed, clearly in no hurry to begin. "It's quite a tale."

His jade-green eyes alight, he contemplated his complex ancestry. At that moment, Lucretia was struck by the realization that he was virtually the ideal man of her fantasies—bronzed and self-assured, indeed commanding, yet generous and sensitive.

Perhaps he was hesitating because he hated to brag. She knew that his mother and his teachers had instilled in Robbie the code of the perfect English gentleman who rarely showed his feelings and never bragged.

"It all began in the autumn of 1956 when the Chinese were wooing the Indians," he finally began. "The Chinese Embassy in New Delhi held a reception, maybe the grandest ever held anywhere. China's Premier Zhou Enlai was already a superstar on the international stage. He was the host. India's Prime Minister Pandit Jawaharlal Nehru, another superstar, was the guest of honor. Neither quite guests nor hosts there were two young 'living Buddhas,' as you call them, reincarnations of past religious leaders. The Dalai Lama and the Panchen Lama were once the first and second men in Tibet, not only living gods, divinities on earth, but politically all-powerful—before the Chinese conquest. They were now exhibited like puppets to the outside world."

The rhythmic cadence of Robbie's words showed that he had told this tale before. His eloquent formal language showed his reverence.

"The setting was magical. Except for the rainbow electric lights sparkling in the trees, it could have been the courtyard of the palace of a Moghul emperor in Delhi centuries earlier. Torches blazed on poles planted in the ground. Unseen musicians played traditional instruments, alternating Indian and Chinese melodies. Floodlights created pools of brilliance, casting the shadowed places into inky darkness. Servants bearing Chinese delicacies wore turbans of gold and scarlet fantastically shaped—like eagles' wings or whales' flukes. All in all, it was uncanny . . . otherworldly.

"Pandit Nehru wore the tight white trousers called jodhpurs and his customary long black tunic with a stand-up collar. As always, a fresh rose was pinned to his breast.

"Zhou Enlai was dashing and dapper. A Mao suit was then obligatory for all in China, Communists, usually dark-blue cotton trousers and jacket buttoned right up to the turned-down collar. That garb demonstrated proletarian austerity, Socialist equality, and Communist lack of pretension by its plainness and its wretched, sloppy tailoring, as well as its wrinkles and its stains. But Zhou Enlai's Mao jacket was beautifully tailored, its immaculate gray-blue tropical worsted knife-edge pressed.

"The Dalai Lama and the Panchen Lama wore formal robes that left their right shoulders bare, one dark crimson, the other saffron. Yet they somehow looked a typical pair off an American campus of the early nineteen-fifties, their hair, cropped to a very short crew cut, enhanced that impression. The bespectacled Dalai looked like a very serious student, but his smile was warm and mischievous. The Panchen, taller and more muscular, was like a football star who was not very good at his studies. His expression was surly and bewildered.

"Then the supporting cast: army, navy, and air force officers of a score of nations in dress uniforms ranging from scarlet to midnight blue, their chests ablaze with medals dangling from rainbow ribbons; diplomats in dinner jackets, miniature decorations bright splotches on their satin lapels; and, of course, hundreds of Indians in a dozen native costumes, the simplest no more than a billowing, voluminous white loincloth worn with a homespun jacket, the most elaborate the parti-colored silks and barbarically splendid jewelry of maharajahs and their ranis.

"Intermingled were the bulbous turbans and the aggressive beards of Sikhs; the tubular longyis and almost transparent blouses of Burmese men and ladies; and the long skirts slit to the waist of the *ao-dai* worn by Vietnamese, both men and women.

"Of course, all the ladies were splendidly arrayed, for the grandest reception of their lives, in gowns and saris of gorgeous many-colored silks, satins, and tulles that shimmered in the torchlight. Fabrics interwoven with gold or silver thread shone in the torches' glare and glowed incandescent when touched by the floodlights."

Embarrassed by his own eloquence, Robbie coughed, and apologized. "Sorry! I'm talking too much."

"No. Hardly." Lucretia replied. "It's fascinating! Please go on."

"Among the lesser guests," he continued, "were Miss Althea Garland, a third secretary attached to the Information Service of the British High Commission, and Colonel Chogal Rabnet, who was the Dalai Lama's closest lay adviser. A hereditary soldier, he was currently assigned to the fearless Khampa warrior-brigands who were rising against Chinese oppression. Otherwise, the entourage of the two living Buddhas were Tibetan lamas, that is, monks in robes shading from deep carmine to canary yellow.

"Althea looked at Chogal oddly. She wondered why such a vital, virile man was wasting his life as a monk. She didn't know that his embossed silk robe and tight green trousers were not a monastic habit, but the formal dress of a Tibetan gentleman.

"So they met. They met, and they talked. Althea Garland was intrigued by the young man in the barbaric costume who was so eloquent in such flawless English. During the last days of the British Raj, when he was very young, Chogal Rabnet had been sent to India to be tutored by a very English lady who had taught a previous Viceroy's children. Settled in Calcutta with her unambitious Bengali husband, who was an unsung poet, she badly needed the generous allowance Chogal's father paid her."

Robbie told Lucretia how the venturesome English miss and the dashing Tibetan colonel had met by stealth immediately after the reception—and had thereafter met repeatedly. Knowing each other for no more than two weeks, they'd been married in secret—ironically for him under the Indian Christian Marriage Act, which covered all who were not Hindus or Muslims. They had married in haste before the departure he could not postpone.

He had not asked the permission of the Dalai Lama; nor had she asked the permission of the High Commissioner, who was the British ambassador and her superior.

"The marriage was frowned upon when Althea finally informed the High Commissioner. The Dalai Lama gave his blessing, but wondered how that new tie to India would affect Colonel Chogal Rabnet's performance as Lhasa's liaison officer to the Khampa's war against the Chinese."

Robbie let that question hang in the air for some twenty seconds before resuming: "Those were very different days, though less than half a century past. The High Commissioner was horrified by Althea Garland's marrying a Tibetan who was not only undeniably non-British, but was, moreover—as British intelligence informed him—a key man in the Mi Mang, the burgeoning Tibetan resistance. Fearing the Chinese would learn of the marriage and vehemently protest the tie between a British diplomat and a Tibetan rebel, the High Commissioner sacked Althea. She was left with no resources except her small savings and the gold coins Chogal sent her from time to time. Having returned to eastern Tibet to rejoin the Mi Mang, he was able to visit her only three times in some sixteen months.

"Nonetheless, Althea refused the passage to England the High Commissioner was bound to offer her. She had no family in England, and she would under no circumstances leave India voluntarily. That would have meant leaving Chogal—and giving up hope of their someday living a normal married life."

"What a wonderful story!" Lucretia sighed. She was charmed and deeply moved by the strange tale and its narrator.

"When Althea wrote Chogal that she was pregnant, his reply

took six weeks to arrive," Robbie continued. "He was ecstatic! He promised he'd somehow get to Delhi for the birth. Six days later, Althea received a letter from the Dalai Lama's unofficial emissary in India. Colonel Chogal Rabnet, it reported with regret, had been killed by mortar shells during a Khampa raid on a Chinese military encampment.

"My father was dead, and my mother was four months pregnant with me. She was almost dead broke and had no prospect of earning anything. What could she possibly do?"

Robbie stood and looked at Lucretia. She was on the verge of tears, her eyes shining and her lower lip trembling. She was, he knew now, not a hardboiled woman of the world but a delightful and vulnerable romantic.

"After much letter-writing and interminable waiting for replies, Althea Garland Rabnet sailed for Hong Kong." Robbie tried to sound matter-of-fact. "But she could just scrape up enough for a second-class passage on a second-class coaster. She'd been promised a job though with the British Information Service in Hong Kong. She knew the director well, having worked with him in Singapore.

"A pariah in India, she was welcomed gladly in Hong Kong. With Colonel Chogal Rabnet lying in an unmarked grave, there was little danger of the Chinese protesting her working for an agency of the Foreign Office. Besides, she was now a local hire on an annual contract, no longer a career officer. Regardless, her new chief wasn't worried about offending the Chinese. His mission was, above all, discrediting Beijing."

"What a wonderful story!" Lucretia sighed. "Does it make you unhappy talking about it?"

"Only that I'd loved to have met my father. Otherwise, it just meant I wasn't born in India, but in Hong Kong thirty-nine years ago. And we stayed. Mum liked it here."

"Can I meet her? She sounds like a lovely lady."

"You can see her, Lucretia, but you can't meet her. She's been a bit gaga for ten years. Premature senile dementia, the doctors call it. No danger of her causing a diplomatic incident now. Any rate, the Hong Kong Regional Information Office disappeared years ago—for fear of offending the Communists!

"She's in the Hong Kong Sanatorium. And she'll die there, but not for a long time. She's fine physically. Only her brain is gone."

"How sad, Robbie. I'm so sorry."

"I still miss her. She's not . . . never . . . there when I go to see her. Only her body, but not herself!" He hurried on. "Regardless, my tale's almost finished. My parents were a lot more interesting than me.

"I studied in Hong Kong at the Island School, right through the sixth form. Mum somehow picked up enough beyond her tiny pension to keep us going. Partly, I learned after she fell ill, by borrowing from old friends. The most generous was old T. Y. Lee of the Bank of Ningpo and Fuchow. A hint of a romance there, though neither would ever say. You know, I've paid back more than half. But I'm getting off the track. . . ."

"How did you get to Imperial College? It's very prestigious, I've heard."

"Best in Europe for engineering, they boast. Almost true, too. I didn't get there until I was in my twenties. Meanwhile, I'd worked on construction sites and road gangs, anything to pick up a few dollars in the building trade. Construction always fascinated me.

"I started as a navvy, a pick and shovel laborer, later worked as a foreman or clerk. Builders in the Colony always need somebody who can write and figure. I'd picked up Cantonese in the streets and Mandarin from the movies. . . . To cut it short, Imperial finally gave me a Lulworth Bursary, a scholarship, you Yanks'd say. And I was on my way."

Lucretia looked down at her hands, which were tightly clasped in her lap, and her dark hair fell across her face. She'd known Robbie was not pretentious, if anything far too modest. But only now did she realize how formidable he was. Smiling gravely, she lifted her head, and her tear-bright eyes looked directly into his.

"Time you got back to the Y," Robbie said. "It'll make your life much easier if you can turn up a suitable flat."

"It'll take a miracle!"

Lucretia said no more, but simply rose and came into his arms. Jacobus protested in his deep bass voice. Each time he barked, his head bobbed, and his tail jerked up and down like a mechanical toy.

They gave Jacobus no further cause for jealousy. Much as she wanted Robbie, Lucretia would not yield to him at this moment. Their lovemaking would have been too quick and too messy if it were shadowed by her need to meet the acquaintance who thought he'd found an apartment she could afford.

Besides, she somehow felt the time was not yet ripe.

6

LUCRETIA COULD NOT recall the number that distinguished the tower where Robbie lived from its seven identical neighbors. She only remembered some kind of eating house on the ground floor. But ground floor shops in every one of the eight towers offered food of every kind from raw or dried to ready to eat.

As he joked, "The Cantonese only care about three things besides getting rich and perpetuating their families: eating, gambling, and . . . ah . . . love."

She smiled at the memory. Robbie had looked startled when she asked, "Do you mean love or bonking?"

After a moment he'd grinned and observed, "That's a very English euphemism. Any rate, bonking is last by a whisker."

Lucretia's humor occasionally was risqué. Anyway, she didn't want Robbie to think her a prude. She'd now been to his apartment three times, each time surprised by his restraint—and a little miffed. Although she'd told him she wasn't yet ready for him, she had half feared—and half hoped—that he'd take her in his arms and ride over her hesitance. Yet he had not so much as touched her except when their hands brushed—and Jacobus the lion dog bellowed in protest.

It was stupid, this coyness of hers, though neither feigned nor meant to tantalize. She was acting like a seventeen-year-old virgin—if there were any seventeen-year-old virgins left. Her reluctance could imperil the bond between them, which was fast becoming the most important thing in the world for her. He was so ardent he could soon tire of a love affair that was intense emotionally and intellectually, yet arid physically. He could end it all in frustration, despite his great affection for her.

She was also frightened of yielding. Suppose she were a drag in bed, disappointing him. Would he turn away, deprive her of his love entirely? Her husband had told her she was like a dead sheep in bed—and had gone off to the eighteen-year-old Chinese tart, definitely no virgin she, he shared with four of his Chinese associates.

No matter how patient Robbie was, no matter how tender and tolerant, he could soon *demand* that they seal their love as lovers had for millennia. Anyway, she wanted him as much as he wanted her, maybe even more. She no longer felt physical revulsion, the clenched stomach and the closed throat, as she had when she first envisioned making love to him. But she was still hanging back.

It was a long time since the first year of her marriage, when a passionate Lawrence Barnes had tumbled her into bed, onto the nearest couch, or even the floor at the oddest times—so often she was always a little sore. She now wanted, needed, a man badly.

Not any man, though. Only Robbie, her Thunderbolt. He had reawakened her sensual nature—and only he could satisfy her. But, she wondered, could she satisfy him?

Quite deliberately, Lucretia thrust aside that anxiety in order to deal with the problem of finding Robbie's building. She shifted the green and white Seibu bag to her left hand. It was heavy, but its contents had not come from the Japanese-owned department store in Pacific Place that dispensed all the luxuries of the world—especially foodstuffs, wines, and liquors—for fantastic prices. She had done her shopping at the Western Market. Robbie had introduced her to that constantly scrubbed yet still squalid emporium, where food cost a third of Seibu's prices.

Yet the slaughterhouse stench of blood and the foul odor of dried fish—pungent, salty, and overripe—was nauseating. Nor could one avoid the reproachful glare of the severed heads hanging above the stalls: grinning pigs, startled steers, and stoic sheep. Yet she could no longer afford Seibu's exorbitant prices—and that was that.

Lucretia walked among the gray towers in hope and finally saw it: the Chinese character she'd learned to find Robbie's building. She saw the glowing, soft red Chinese character for *jook:* the symbol for rice flanked by two archers' bows. Thick rice gruel made with chicken or fish stock, jook came with delicious tidbits: from fresh peanuts and sweet Cantonese sausages to pickled mustard greens and eggs preserved in lime, which foreigners called hundred-year-old eggs—and stupidly shunned.

The pale red-neon jook grew misty before her eyes. Suddenly it gleamed bright scarlet and terrifyingly began to expand. Its sinuous lines were now writhing, fiery snakes with distended jaws flashing great fangs. Bursting through the plate-glass, the snakes grew bigger and bigger until they were as enormous as burning telephone poles. They reared to coil around her shoulders, to envelope and consume her.

Lucretia was paralyzed, unable even to scream. Looking around wildly, she saw the open doorway of the eating house, at once inviting and sinister. At last she screamed, shrill and hoarse. The pedestrians around the gray tower stared in astonishment as she dashed through the doorway.

Slumping exhausted into a chair, she knew the snakes no longer pursued her. But malevolent faces leered in the doorway: evil dwarves, maimed soldiers, and malformed giants, all gibbering threats.

A tremor shook her violently, and her teeth chattered uncontrollably. The flaming snakes were invading her refuge. Overcome by fear, she shuddered and closed her eyes. But the snakes still writhed on the inside of her eyelids, hissing hideously.

When she opened her eyes, she saw the cook-waitress standing over her. Still trembling, she forced a smile. It must have come out a menacing grimace, for the woman shrank back. The next instant, however, she shyly stroked Lucretia's arm.

"All right, Missy, all right," the woman murmured and placed a cup of tea in Lucretia's hands. "All soon be fine."

Already a little calmer, Lucretia sipped the bitter tea. She smiled tremulously at concern for a stranger.

Her benefactors were chatting animatedly. She heard the words *taksi,* meaning taxi. She shook her head and said, *"Mgoi, myew taksi!"*

Patrons and waitress gasped in astonishment. The mad foreign woman actually spoke a few words of an intelligible language.

"No, thank you," she had said, almost exhausting her Cantonese vocabulary. "I don't need a taxi."

Lucretia knew just what had happened to her, and she knew

it was now all over. The doctors called it by various names: panic attack, anxiety incident, acute disorientation, or tropical neuraesthenia. She'd heard that last term in New Delhi on a business trip with Lawrence.

"Tropical neuraesthenia," the doctor of the British High Commission had explained to a dinner party. "Americans get it worst, especially underemployed wives with ten servants they don't know what to do with. Their husbands work in nice clean air-conditioned offices, but the ladies, God bless them, go out to see India.

"Take a lady who's away from God's country for the first time and is filling her idle hours shopping in Connaught Circus for gifts for the folks at home. The sun is molten—merciless. It's so hot cars're stuck in the melting tarmacadam. She sees only strange brown faces. She's assailed by foul stenches. Garbage is piled up everywhere, all terribly unsanitary. Everything is a hazard to health and sanity.

"She rushes into a shop to escape. And she sees more of those leering brown faces gibbering in their weird language. She trembles and sees danger everywhere. It's all too much for her!

"If it continues, she and her husband are med-evaced, sent home. If she gets over it, she's all right."

Recalling that little lecture, Lucretia knew she was now truly all right. It was only a mild attack, though it hadn't seemed mild a few minutes ago. She'd had a much more virulent attack just after arriving in Hong Kong for the first time. And a milder attack when she'd first contemplated sleeping with Robbie. The connection with today's attack was clear.

She proffered a ten-dollar note for the tea, but the waitress pushed it back. You didn't need Cantonese to know she was saying she could not take money from the poor sick lady. What had she done? Only a cup of tea!

Lucretia smiled her thanks, picked up the heavy Seibu bag, and walked out the door. The jook symbol was now its normal size, glowing pale red. It was humdrum, no longer menacing, hardly worth noticing.

LUCRETIA PUSHED THE button marked 34, and the twin doors of the elevator snapped shut with a metallic clang. During the rapid ascent her hands were busy with comb, mirror, and lipstick, repairing the ravages of the panic attack. Though painful, it was a cleansing, even illuminating experience. She now understood her reluctance to consummate her love for Robbie—and she had almost decided what she would now do. But, she nonetheless wondered about the likelihood of this thunderbolt love's enduring. To placate her stern conscience she had to believe they would remain together for a long, long time.

When the elevator doors slammed open, Lucretia tucked lipstick, comb, and mirror into the capacious leather pouch dangling from her arm. She picked up the Seibu bag, pasted a smile on her face, and stepped onto the landing opposite the little plaque on the much locked grill marked 34-A.

Robbie kissed her lightly on the cheek after opening the door and laboriously unlocking the protective grill. The small air conditioner in the casement window was overworked in the intense heat that was somewhat unusual for late September. It wheezed and coughed and grudgingly puffed cooled air into the small living room. Occasionally, it shuddered and rattled, all but stopped, and then cut in again.

Robbie sprawled in the easy chair opposite the window. His

long legs were sheathed in faded jeans, his feet in gleaming loafers, and his torso in a white T-shirt. Looking younger than his thirty-nine years, he might at first glance have been a graduate student or a youngish Ivy League professor. A second glance, however, revealed a quite unacademic face, which was like a sword. His aquiline nose was the blade, his green eyes jewels on the hilt.

"I really should get a new one." He nodded at the laboring air conditioner. "It sounds like a small steamer in a big storm. Every once in a while it heaves its screw out of the water, threatens to capsize—and at the last minute plops back into the water."

"Why don't you?" Lucretia asked idly. "It'd be a welcome relief."

"Poverty, my dear! I can't afford a new one."

"Robbie, why ever not? You can get a reconditioned machine for a thousand Hong Kong. Not much more than a hundred US."

"I haven't got a thousand. I'm not overpaid, you know."

"Why not get another job?"

He only shrugged, and she persisted, "Employers're begging for skilled employees. Warm bodies to replace all those clever midlevel Chinese managers and professionals who're taking off for more salubrious parts."

"More than a half million've left already. But what's that to do with me?"

"Americans, Aussies, and Brits're doing work foreigners never did before, jobs foreigners disdained before. The Colony is labor short. A lad from Liverpool called me yesterday . . . wanted to fix my plumbing in my own language. I could hardly understand a word he said. Anyway, I told him the house committee looked after the plumbing in my new apartment."

"I'm happy enough with Granger, Reynolds, and O'Dowd."

Robbie brushed her suggestion aside. "I know where I am with them. And nobody's rushing to start up as chartered surveyors with hardly more than a year to go before the Chinese . . ."

Lucretia ached to press her point. But she knew from the slight curl of his lips and the negligent wave of his hand that it was hopeless. Though not often stubborn, Robbie was most stubborn when most casual. Passive was the last word anyone would apply to him. Yet he was content, though scandalously underpaid. And that was that! He also stonewalled on anything to do with the coming takeover, shutting her out and saying, "I won't stick my neck out again."

Yet he knew full well that he did not fit the Hong Kong pattern. As he pointed out, "I'm not Cantonese or Shanghainese or Beijingese, not even Chinese. And I'm not really English, not a European. But I'm still a barbarian, a *gwaitau,* a foreign devil-head, to the clannish Chinese. Also a Tibetan halfbreed—and poor into the bargain."

He now smiled, not bitter, only detached. He could laugh at himself and his predicament. Since he would do exactly as he pleased, Lucretia told herself to relax.

The long summer twilight flaunted its pink and violet cloak over the harbor, and the neon signs were just coming on in Kowloon side. That spectacle she saw from the kitchen window, which offered the only view in the apartment, while she was preparing dinner.

They were staying in tonight because she was tired after moving her belongings from the YWCA to the new apartment. The Y, despite its name, was anything but austere. It was rather like a luxurious small hotel. But she could no longer afford US$100 a day, which was moderate for Hong Kong.

She'd been very lucky to find the apartment—and stupendously lucky to get it free, even to a Filipina maid, paying only for utilities and telephone. But that great piece of luck had taken a long time to materialize. She'd answered dozens of ads, even put an ad of her own in the *South China Morning Post.* Almost everything had been beyond her slender means, even an offer to share an apartment with a middle-aged English lady and her elderly lover. What was not pricey was revolting.

She had finally stumbled upon this treasure through a colleague at the Chinese University who suggested, "Try Ted Tomlinson. He's helping out the Physics Department, but he works for one of those big, go-ahead scientific firms. He's going to MIT for a course, and he's looking for a flat-sitter. Doesn't want to leave the place unwatched for months. He won't charge. His firm pays the rent and the maid."

Lucretia relished the enticing fragrance of garlic, parsley, oregano, and roasting chicken wafted from the kitchen, where she had been busy with her purchases from Western Market. She had kept Robbie out with dire threats. Obediently, he now sat in the easy chair, sipping a San Miguel beer and drinking in the music.

Having lived amid luxury and turmoil for three years, she found that modest domestic scene pleasant. She poured a little vodka over the ice cubes in her squat tumbler, added water and lime juice, then settled on the sofa to enjoy the music and the peace. She could not see the theatrical sunset over the harbor, but her view of Robbie's profile more than made up for it.

His lean jaw was a long sharp line against the fading light from the closed casement window. Although he had not shaved today, it was virtually free of stubble. He would have liked to grow a beard that would hide the delightful line of his jaw. Fortunately, his facial hair was too sparse.

Robbie was wholly at ease, his hands lying relaxed on his thighs. They were good hands, powerful, competent, and beautifully shaped—sensitive as well as sensual. They might have been carved of tawny marble by an ancient Greek sculptor. She thought of those hands on her body and suppressed a shiver.

Sitting quietly for fifteen minutes or so, Lucretia sipped her vodka. From time to time one of them threw out a brief remark, and the other replied as briefly. No need for words just now. Though they had on occasion talked half the night away, this evening they were both content with long silences.

Lucretia rose, refilled her glass, doling out another small tot of vodka, and found a beer for Robbie. She sat and sipped again, her foot keeping time to the music. With sudden decision, she tossed down the remaining vodka and lime, throwing her head back to catch the last drops. She shivered slightly when the intense cold in her mouth was succeeded by a flush of warmth in her belly.

Abruptly, she rose again and made for the minute kitchen, mumbling about looking at the chicken. He nodded abstractedly and picked up the *Hong Kong Standard*.

After a few minutes she emerged and pulled the kitchen door closed behind her. Carrying her all-purpose leather pouch, which was a shade too businesslike for her frivolous violet sundress, she made for the mirror in the small bedroom.

"Robbie, I need your help," she called, her right hand emerging from the pouch with a piece of jewelry.

"You've got to help me decide. This brooch was locked in the safe at the Y. I forgot about it until I moved, but the desk clerk gave it to me."

"Very pretty." He glanced perfunctorily at the sunburst of semiprecious gems set in pink gold. "What's the problem?"

"It was my mother's. A little old-fashioned now, I'm afraid. Anyway, I'd like your opinion. Does it do anything for me? Or should I sell it? Though the sentimental value's . . ."

"Bring you more in London or New York than Hong Kong," he said. "It's a buyer's market here."

"Wai Kee, the jewelers, are interested."

"They say you can trust Wai Kee. But why ask me something I know nothing about?"

"That's not what I'm asking, you jerk. I want to know how it looks on me. Come here, and I'll show you."

Robbie stood behind Lucretia and gazed gravely at their reflection in the long mirror on the wall across from the big bed.

Lucretia lifted the brooch and held it to the shoulder strap of her dress. When he laid his hands lightly on her shoulders, she neither frowned nor moved away. She only smiled and asked, "Or would it go better here?"

She shifted the brooch to her waist, and held it there for a moment. Stepping backward and closer to him, she moved the brooch to the swell of a breast and asked, "Or is it better here? More provocative?"

Clasping her waist, Robbie asked with a conspiratorial half smile, "What *are* you trying to do, madam?"

"Why, nothing," she answered. "Just getting your opinion of the brooch."

He spun her around and kissed her urgently, his hands hard

on her back. Lucretia shivered with pleasure and whispered, "I'm also trying to seduce you. How am I doing?"

"You're doing beautifully, full marks," he whispered, adding after an instant: "I hate to be practical, but what about Jacobus? We don't want him bellowing at us."

"Oh, Jacobus!" She smiled. "He's had a good dinner . . . should be content locked in the kitchen. But, just to be sure, I gave him a big, juicy shinbone."

7

THEIR FIRST ENCOUNTER in bed was not much like the ecstasies imagined by the authors of adult romances when heroine and hero know each other wholly for the very first time. Nor was it the rapturous sunburst that lyric poets hymn, revealing glorious new worlds. The earth did not move, and they were not lifted to a higher plane.

In truth, it was a bit awkward. They fumbled with each other's clothes almost as clumsily as ardent teenagers with shaking hands. It was, Lucretia reflected fleetingly, a blessing that one wore so little in the unseasonable blast furnace heat of Hong Kong in late September. She was wearing no more than a gauzy sundress, and two wisps of undergarments, which she left for Robbie to remove after he slipped out of his jeans and T-shirt.

She felt his heart drumming when he pulled her close. Her

own heart was beating just as eagerly. Yet they were inhibited: a first encounter could go terribly wrong. Despite their sophistication, they were also inhibited by lingering shyness.

The small bedroom was sweltering in the humidity-saturated late afternoon heat. It boasted no air conditioner, and the closed door shut off the cool air from the wheezy air conditioner in the living room.

Slick with sweat, their bodies glided over and around each other—and that natural lubrication was intensely erotic. When they were at last joined, their bellies smacked wetly against each other—and parted with a report like a champagne cork when they drew away momentarily.

Lucretia felt herself rising toward the heights. It had been so long, so many years, since she had made love wholeheartedly. Her body disregarded the difficulties and the absurdities of this eager coupling. She felt herself rising like a skyrocket. When it came, the explosion was rather brief and rather slight. But it was not paltry, it was her first in ages.

Robbie exploded inside her with a hoarse cry. She was in no mind to resent the all but guaranteed male orgasm. Not when the male concerned had just lifted her almost, though not quite, to the stars.

Until sheer sensation submerged all distractions, Robbie had been distracted by his fear that Jacobus would weary of the shinbone and bellow protests at his imprisonment. Even less rationally, Lucretia had been fearful that the lion dog would somehow break out and invade their sanctuary.

She was also distracted by her anxiety to please Robbie. She had to prove to him—and thus to herself—that she was not at all like a dead sheep in bed. That accusation of Lawrence Barnes hurt most. No more did Robbie confide to Lucretia that her eagerness, her all but aggressiveness, had startled him, almost put him off.

Beyond need for words, they went hand-in-hand into the living room, which the old air conditioner had brought down to a reasonably comfortable temperature as the late afternoon wore into twilight. He wore a checked cotton Indonesian sarong and had given her a Japanese yukata, a soft cotton garment like a bathrobe.

The light from the sky was reflected down the well between the windows of the apartments, at first delicate mauve, a faint, almost transparent blend of pink and blue. At the close of the subtropical twilight, the sky flushed a glowing violet and rapidly turned purple. The finale of that blessed day was the fall of a dense, almost opaque, indigo curtain.

Robbie drifted into the kitchen and returned with tall glasses of iced white wine and soda. They sat close together on the small couch, her head on his shoulder. His thumb stroked her nipple lazily, while her forefinger traced abstract patterns on his smooth bronzed chest. Freed from his prison, Jacobus watched benevolently—and silently.

"You see, he's accepted you," Robbie said. "No more barking."

"I should hope so—after I gave my all—made the greatest sacrifice a woman can."

"If that's the way you feel . . . " he bantered. "Why, we just won't do it again, not ever. I promise."

"You'd better do it again, if you know what's good for you," she replied. "You know, I might just get to like this exercise, sweaty as it is."

Lucretia looked long and hard at Robbie, as if seeing him for the first time. He returned her intent gaze, as if seeing her for the first time. Everything was different now.

She saw his strong features completely relaxed for the first time since she'd known him. He seemed to glow. Above the heavy cheekbones that framed his hawk's beak nose, his green eyes were no longer piercing, but gentle. His wide mouth was soft, no longer set in conscious firmness. She had never noticed how sensuous was his full lower lip.

Robbie saw a slender woman whose matte white skin was flushed with pleasure, her normally pale-blue eyes still dark with passion. She brushed her tousled black hair off her forehead with the back of her hand and smiled at him, tender and triumphant. The faint fullness around her mouth, now free of lipstick, was sensual and seductive.

Their gentle caresses became stronger, first tentative, then eager and finally urgent. Shedding their simple garments, they drew together again on the couch. An instant later they faced each other standing, brightly lit by the living room lamps against the curtain of night.

Their renewed lovemaking was frenzied and lasted far longer. Enclasped, they whirled about the room, falling first onto the couch and then onto the dragon carpet. They offered each other complex caresses, yet neither said a word. The only sound was their kisses, their rapid breathing, and the no longer gentle smack of flesh on flesh. Through slitted eyelids she looked up at his face, which was set in a triumphant grimace though his eyes were shut. He was at once very close and far away.

When he entered her, Lucretia no longer felt the prickle of the Tibetan carpet on her back and shoulders. All her senses were fixed on Robbie and the unimaginable sensations he drew from her. Almost too quickly, she soared, and soared, and soared into the heavens, enfolded by the sky's indigo darkness. When the skyrockets exploded, she knew nothing but the surge and the surge, and the opening and the opening of all her senses, soaring upward and upward.

Later she asked, "Was it all right for you? I couldn't tell."

He grinned and said, "How could you notice anything? You were making so much noise I thought we'd have the fire brigade in. No, it was *not* all right. It was splendid . . . wonderful!"

Lucretia all but blushed. It might take longer to bring her to orgasm than it did him, though not always, and it was not certain every time. But, by the Lord, when she did, she exploded with delight, all her being brilliantly alight and vibrantly alive. He had restored her feminine confidence, her sense of herself as an accomplished and loving woman. She now knew that she could give a man great pleasure, total fulfillment. She knew too that she was capable of feeling great pleasure herself—overwhelming fulfillment.

A pity that Lawrence Barnes would never know that his dead sheep was actually a sensual tigress!

THE NEXT MONTH WAS always to be to Lucretia "the idyllic time," the most perfect spell of joy in her life. She had joined her body to Robbie's, and nothing could go wrong in the enchanted days that followed.

The idyll began with the Mid-Autumn Festival, the age-old celebration of the fullness of the land and gathering of the crops. That evening at the end of September was the first day of the harvest festival. Although only a fraction of Hong

Kong's valuable land still produced crops, everyone was in a holiday mood. The festive atmosphere was irresistible when Lucretia and Robbie left the apartment block, drunk with their own joy.

An orange moon hung over Kowloon across the bay, so low that it was partly hidden behind the hills: the edges of the peaks were jagged, as if nibbled by heavenly mice. Entranced, they watched the moon shake off the clutching hills to hang an immense glowing platter against the sky. The rivers of bright headlights flowing through the thoroughfares of Kowloon were streaked red by thousands of tail lights.

Robbie saw in the moon two figures celebrated in myth: the rabbit that has always lived there and the court lady who was exiled there after a disastrous love affair. He was nonplussed when Lucretia saw neither. She saw only the face of the man in the moon.

Abrim with happiness, Robbie was for an instant chilled. It was not simply that Lucretia and he had been taught since infancy to see different beings in the moon. So many everyday sights and actions had different meanings for them, as if they had grown up on different planets. Still, he reassured himself, he could see the man in the moon, as well as the rabbit and the maiden. His English mother had seen to that, while laughing with him at the old belief that the moon was made of green cheese. Asia and the West—he had footholds in both camps. Lucretia now had to learn to move easily between those camps—and that would take time.

He, of course, knew the associations the harvest festival evoked for her. Who did not know in an era shaped by American television and movies? Thanksgiving, two months later than the moon festival, evoked pilgrims in stovepipe hats and Indians in feathered headdresses, as well as golden brown roast turkeys and tart red cranberry sauce. Also the pungent smoke of bonfires of fallen leaves rising under chill skies. Americans even had a different name for the season. They called it not autumn, but fall.

How much did Lucretia know of the harvest season in Asia? Of course, the Chinese character for autumn showed fire burning off the stubble left by the harvest. How near the concepts, and how far apart their forms and the images they evoked!

First came mooncakes, flaky pastries as round as the harvest moon, which were filled with almond paste, glazed chestnuts, hardboiled eggs, and candied lotus seeds. Hong Kong might fly the Union Jack—for the next year or so—but the warp and woof of the Hong Kong in which he'd grown up were Chinese. Holidays, food, customs, family relations—all were in the Chinese manner, a little modified in the Colony.

The moon festival also recalled the day in A.D. 1368 when the Chinese rose against their Mongol rulers and brought down the mighty dynasty of Kubilai Khan. The secret messages that linked the conspirators were concealed in mooncakes, since no Mongol guard would be suspicious of that festive pastry. And colored lanterns had signaled the moment for the rising.

Therefore Western-educated Chinese in the British Crown Colony of Hong Kong six centuries later ate mooncakes to commemorate that revolt, and their children paraded with globular lanterns. The Chinese had long memories.

LUCRETIA LIKED TO roll the phrase on her tongue: "the idyllic time," the month or so when nothing could touch the happiness that enveloped Robbie and herself. Nothing, not even the great divergence between their fundamental beliefs: her old New England conviction of the supreme power of words, ideas, and logic; his weird amalgam of solid John Bull common sense with uncanny Tibetan mysticism.

Robbie was a hard-headed engineer. He dealt with solid realities he could see, touch, and measure, not with myths or fantasies. Yet his faith, the core of his being, was committed to an ideal that was both abstract and fanciful. He believed that pure virtue existed on earth, that yearning toward goodness was inborn in every human being.

The Buddhist practice of releasing live birds and fish to gain merit was, he contended, purely altruistic. The unselfish goodness of an elect few, he went on, would over the centuries inspire ever more human beings to behave virtuously toward both animals and mankind. There was a touch of the Buddha in all of us, though some had been touched more deeply by the lord of evil.

Eating neither meat nor fish was the logical conclusion of the Buddhist belief that all living beings possessed individual souls. Those souls passed into other animals or into new humans after the death of the body they had inhabited. Good Buddhists should therefore eat only vegetables. Otherwise, they could be responsible for killing a yak or a chicken whose soul had passed from a human, perhaps a cousin or parent of the meat-eater. Yet, in the harsh climate of the high Tibetan plateau, few could practice vegetarianism.

Those strong enough in spirit to abstain, Robbie said, were greatly honored, which showed how few they were. Those who butchered animals for others to eat were shunned, which showed how perverse human beings were, even devout Buddhists. Most

Tibetans happily consumed meat when they could get it—and scorned those who provided it.

Robbie was thus tough-minded in judging his fellow humans, Buddhist or Christian, Taoist or Confucian. Yet he inhabited a spiritual realm of insubstantial, always shifting, lights and shadow. The complexity of Tantric Buddhism made Western religions seem straightforward and lacking in nuance. Robbie revered a host of otherworldly beings, hundreds of diverse divinities. When he remembered, he was also wary of a horde of evil demons.

Tantric Buddhism promised Nirvana to those who attained enlightenment by profound study culminating in divine inspiration. Also by giving up all desire. He said he was a bad candidate for Nirvana because he was athrob with desire for Lucretia and for all the worldly goods he wanted to give her.

Nirvana was not a conventional heaven of perfect pleasure for every individual soul. It was a rarefied nonbeing that merged the individual soul with the essential stuff of the universe—when matter and spirit became indistinguishable.

Above all, Robbie revered bodhisattvas, the most virtuous and the most worldly of Buddhist divinities. Bodhisattvas had attained enlightenment, but chose to remain outside Nirvana until all living beings were enlightened. Above all, they helped others attain Nirvana. Most widely worshiped in Asia was the bodhisattva Guan Yin, known as the Goddess of Mercy. That female deity succored women, giving them good husbands and many children. As the Blessed Virgin Mary was to Catholics, she was to Buddhists from Tibet and Mongolia to China, Japan, and Vietnam. Guan Yin was always serene and always responsive, rarely leaving prayers unanswered.

Lucretia was delighted by the poetic imagery of Tantric Buddhism, having read widely on that religion. But she drew back from discussing Robbie's faith before the discussion became acrimonious. She would not tax him with the pornographic images lamas used in their spiritual exercises, ostensibly to harden them against desire. Nor would she allude to the lamas' accumulation of land and treasure. She would not tell him that the *sangha* of Tantric Buddhism was no more unsullied and unselfish than was any other old established church. She would certainly not point out that the lamas had exploited the people, though hardly as savagely as Chinese propaganda charged or as cruelly as the Chinese themselves now exploited Tibetans.

Lucretia could say almost anything to Robbie, as long as she did not try to draw him out on Chinese oppression of Tibet or the future of Hong Kong under China. Still, she knew better than to push a presumably abstract discussion to the brink.

Anyway, she loved Robbie as he was. If she talked him into doubting his creed, he would be quite another person—and that she could not bear.

Nonetheless she opened her mind, as well as her heart, to Robbie without reserve. She no longer regarded most men as implacable enemies—and her own man as a potential enemy. The emotional scars left by her years with Lawrence Barnes were now fading from angry red to pink.

She felt a whole person for the first time in years: liberated from the materialistic concentration and the conventional opinions imposed by her marriage. In that new freedom, her spirit soared like a sailplane on fresh winds.

Lucretia gloried in her rousing arguments with Robbie, even in their vigorous disagreements, just as she did in their lovemaking. Both the sensual embraces and the intellectual bouts were delightful and exhilarating in themselves. Both further restored the self-assurance her ex-husband had relentlessly ground down.

And Robbie? For the first time in his adult life he could speak from the heart without fearing ridicule or betrayal. He felt he was a whole man for the first time in his thirty-nine years. He no longer doubted himself or deprecated his achievements because the colonial elite looked down on him. He knew his own worth—in good part because Lucretia valued him so highly.

IT WAS A long climb up splintered wooden stairs lit by dust-covered twenty-five watt bulbs hanging from frayed cords. On the last cramped landing, a scarred wooden door stood ajar.

"Are we really there?" Lucretia asked. "I should've worn mountain boots instead of heels."

"It's only three flights, darling. And they're your friends," Robbie replied. "Anyway, it's good that they're celebrating the day!"

"The day?"

"It's Chung Yeung, remember? The day people climb as high as they can . . . always a month after the Mid-Autumn Festival."

"Of course. Everybody's streaming up the Peak. All because some old fellow centuries ago led his family up a mountain after a soothsayer told him some disaster would hit his village in the valley."

"Disaster, flood or whatever, catastrophe did strike," Robbie said. "But that family was safe."

"So Hong Kong climbs as high as it possibly can once a year. Tradition's nice, even when it's a little screwy."

Light seeped through the cracks between the door and its frame. Through the same cracks floated the dust-and-brown sugar fragrance of incense, as well as the strains of a Mozart violin concerto played on a CD. Also, naturally, the babble of conversation.

It was that kind of party, Robbie decided, opening the door. He'd been to many like it in London, though to none in Hong Kong since his return. It was the kind of party to which you brought your own drink. The plastic bag with three bottles of good white wine clinked at his side.

The guests would be oldish graduate students who worked by day and studied by night; youngish faculty, still abrim with idealism; pro bono lawyers inflating their recent cases; greenies resting between crusades; and a sprinkling of artsy-craftsy types; even some true authorities on Asian art. Also a gaggle of newspapermen, some already half seas over, and a couple of heavyweights from the Democratic Party, which was striving to preserve some measure of popular rule after the Communist deluge.

Pushing the door open for Lucretia, Robbie reflected that there would soon be no more parties like this. Even today, more than eight months before the legions of Beijing were to march in singing "Hong Kong, We Love You," this mildly nonconformist gathering was discreet, for it was held in one of the decrepit old structures that leaned wearily over Hollywood Road, apparently on the verge of collapse. The curio and knickknack center of the Colony was almost deserted after eleven o'clock.

Nor was he likely to meet any of the wealthy Chinese motherland lovers against whose tittle-tattle his honorary uncle, old T. Y. Lee, had warned him. None of the intellectuals and pseudo-intellectuals here tonight would report his continuing association with Lucretia Barnes, whom some considered a notorious right-wing radical!

Beijing's informers were generally not the poor or the middle class, who, in theory, had least to lose by Communist rule. In fact, that group supported the limited democracy the present British governor sponsored. Beijing's staunchest allies were rich entrepreneurs, and their henchmen, like Lawrence Barnes and H. K. Lam.

Robbie felt a stab of guilt. He had, at the very beginning, promised himself that his first date with Lucretia would be his last. Then the second date, which he again swore would be the last. He had finally abandoned prudence when he asked her to his flat in a development crammed with freelance informers.

It was now too late. The more he saw of Lucretia, the more in love with her he was—and the angrier he grew at the threat to his work and his mission. He was now aggressively, though perhaps not wisely, contemptuous of the threat. He was defiant and reckless.

But he could relax tonight. This haphazard collection of Britons, Americans, Australians, and local Chinese would almost all dislike the prospect of Beijing's rule.

Nonetheless he was astonished when he entered the apartment. His expectations regarding his fellow guests were generally correct. But the apartment was very different from the dingy loft the decrepit staircase had led him to expect.

Indirect lighting glowed on blue-and-white Ming Dynasty porcelains displayed in rosewood bookcases. A spotlight illuminated a two-foot-high Tang Dynasty statuette of a camel. Exquisite ancestor portraits of a senior mandarin and his wife recalled his first sight of Lucretia, who was then watching a photographer strive to make a callow shop assistant and his trainee-beautician girlfriend look like an imperial prince and his concubine.

Robbie understood when he saw the magazines *Arts of Asia* and *Architectural Digest* lying beside catalogues of art auctions on a side table. The narrow street-entrance to the staircase, he remembered, was beside a shop protected by steel shutters as tight as a tortoise's shell. The signboard read: THE TREASURY: ANTIQUES, ART, AND ODDITIES. He recalled Lucretia's talking about an American couple who ran the most interesting antique shop in Hong Kong.

She'd told him that their apartment above the shop was not only a magic cave of *objets d'art,* but was one of the most hospitable dwellings in the Colony. The warmth—emotional and physical—drew Robbie in. A charming pastel-painted, half-life-size wooden statue of Guan Yin, the Goddess of Mercy, unusually sensual, welcomed guests. Even the floor coverings were remarkable: an old-gold Tientsin carpet delicately embossed with bamboo leaves; a very old off-white Peking carpet strewn with traditional symbols for luck; and a glowing orange, red, and yellow runner from Central Asia that connected the drawing room and the dining room.

Robbie was overwhelmed by the wealth of prints, paintings, black-ink sketches, and calligraphic scrolls on the walls. He saw Lucretia kissing a slender, gray-haired woman in a red silk caftan, evidently their hostess. She gestured vaguely and said, "Small chow and booze over there. Lucretia, stay and gossip with me!"

Jostling and apologizing, stumbling over outstretched feet, dodging glowing cigarettes, Robbie made for the laden altar table. A bartender in a white jacket drew the cork of one of Robbie's bottles with professional deftness and poured the wine into a crystal tumbler. Robbie congratulated himself on resisting his inclination to buy cheap plonk to a bring-your-own-bottle shindig. Penfold Chardonnay was not costly, but neither was it plonk.

This group was hardly rich, but all things were relative in Hong Kong, especially wealth. Antique dealers, professors, and journalists on, say US$150,000 a year were virtually impoverished beside a US$2-million-a-year family. The US$2-million-a-year family felt poor beside billionaires who were among the ten richest in the world. But even this group could afford the best food and drink available in the Colony, which meant the best in the entire world.

The spread on the altar table beside the bar made ludicrous the Hong Kong term for hors d'oeuvres or snacks, which was small chow. First was the lavish array of dim sum, heart-touchers, as the Cantonese called the tidbits they loved: *shaomai,* little dough purses filled with chopped pork and spiced greens; *hagao,* translucent half-moon shrimp dumplings; tiny meatballs; curried squid tentacles; stewed chicken feet; shrimp fried in rice paper; spring rolls; even costly ducks' tongues—something for everyone and some things some wouldn't touch.

Robbie snaffled two pieces of sushi which included *maguro,* much prized tuna, as well as sea urchin, and golden salmon caviar. Also on the altar table was a fringe of Western delicacies: *paté de foie gras,* smoked salmon coronets filled with *créme fraîche* and black caviar, oysters on the half shell, and lobster in a rich golden mayonnaise. For those who might find that spread inadequate, chafing dishes offered Indonesian and Thai curries.

Tucking four maguro rolls into a napkin for Lucretia, who

loved sushi, Robbie inspected the bar. All the wines were superior to his own good little Chardonnay. The Bordeaux and the Burgundies, which bore famous labels from Château Talbot to Romanée-Conti, were set beside Grange Hermitage, Australia's finest red. The Scotch and bourbon were also top of the line: Laphroaig and Chivas Regal, Jack Daniel's and Jim Beam. He also saw with pleasure a silver cooler of beer: Tsingtao, Heineken, Foster's, and Carlsberg.

Robbie normally drank beer, largely because it fitted his pocket. But he could not resist a really good Scotch, like the eighteen-year-old J&B he spied on the bar. Since the bartender was busy concocting something outlandish with cream, grenadine, and vodka, Robbie poured himself a stiff five ounces. After a moment's reflection, he decided it would be criminal to dilute such splendid whiskey with water or ice. Instead, he drank an ounce or so, savoring the smooth texture, and filled his glass again.

What the hell! the normally abstemious Robbie told himself. A man's got to relax sometime.

An emergency bottle of Tsingtao beer clutched in one hand in case the J&B ran out, he wandered through the spacious flat, enjoying the paintings and idly looking for Lucretia. He was diverted by a stunning woman with flaming red hair, who was seated on a sofa under a highly colored modern Chinese primitive. The skintight sheath of green silk she wore was rucked high up her thighs.

The redhead stretched out a long white arm to snare Robbie's sleeve and demanded, "Now who are you, mate? I haven't seen you before, more's the pity."

Robbie told her his name. She smiled devastatingly and said, "Everybody calls me Blue."

That nickname was assuredly Australian. If her hair were jet black, the same contrarian humor would call her Snowy.

"We were talking about the scourge," she said. "You ought to know about it. What the hell are you anyway?"

"Mostly Tibetan. What's your scourge? Polluting the rivers, fishing out the seas, global warming, mad cow disease, or hormone-fed chickens?"

The woman called Blue smiled broadly and half-slurred, "You've got the right idea, Dorje mate. But that's not the worst of it. Worst is Americanization, making the whole world eat, drink, dress, think, and talk exactly the same way. Independent standards? Bugger 'em! Spiritual values, not materialistic? Screw 'em! Music that's not screaming fits or bloody country and western? Sod it! Everything's got to be the same—just like bloody America."

"Blue, you know goddamned well that's a lotta bullshit!" a tall, bulky young man, American by his accent, protested loudly. He had doffed the jacket that presumably went with his dark trousers, but not the striped rep tie slotted into his blue-Oxford button-down collar.

"You progressive creeps love to badmouth Uncle Sam and the big bad exploiting Yanks," he declared. "But you don't turn down Yankee trade or Yankee protection. What've you got to offer instead of American popular culture, 'Waltzing Matilda'?"

"Don't come the raw prawn on me, Ted!" the redhead directed mystifyingly. "God save me from money traders like you. Not a brain in a carload. Just big balls and bigger mouths."

"Shove it, Blue!" the American advised. "Right where it'll hurt most."

Robbie felt the warmth of the Scotch in his belly, took another long sip, and said mildly, "You know, chum, you're proving the lady's point. You Yanks always shout. But you're not going to make the world one big Disneyland. Not if I can help it!"

"Tibetan you said, didn't you, buddy? What's the Dalai Lama gonna do? Send a couple of his aircraft carriers? You can shove it, too!"

Aware that the Scotch was undermining his normal restraint, Robbie did not reply.

"And what're you, Mac, besides a long way from Tibet?" the aggressive American demanded. "A stooge of the Limeys by your fucking accent. Or a running dog of the Commies. Which is it, boy?"

Robbie turned away, through the American taunted, "Don't you hear me, boy? You ashamed? Scared to answer?"

"Now look here, laddie, let's drop it," Robbie turned again and retorted. "You're full of crap and full of booze. I don't want to hurt you."

Robbie was suddenly aware that Lucretia was standing behind the American, looking incredulous.

"All right, fellows, let's break it up," she said. "That's enough."

The currency trader did not back off, but elbowed Robbie. Caught off guard, Robbie staggered and almost fell. When the American grappled with him, Robbie caught the overpowering stench of alcohol on his breath.

Wondering if his own breath were as foul, Robbie thrust out his elbows and broke the hold. He stepped back, happy to end the incident with that. But the American advanced again—and Robbie drove a short sharp punch into his stomach. His assailant abruptly sat down on the floor.

"Let's get out of here!" Lucretia whispered, taking his arm in a public show of solidarity. "That'll do for tonight!"

"I'm sorry, darling," Robbie apologized as the door closed behind them. "He jumped me. You saw it. But I wouldn't've hit him so hard if I'd known he was dead drunk."

Lucretia took the creaking stairs slowly, pausing at the next landing to say, "No need to talk about it. Sure, I feel humiliated. You didn't have to prove to me you're no pussycat. But what else could . . ."

8

LUCRETIA NOW KNEW that her lover was not always gentle. He could be provoked. More dangerous, the new Robbie was also more impressive. She could hardly reproach him strongly for the brawl, but she did say, "If you must fight, fight for me. Not for some carrot-topped Aussie tart! Not over a stupid attack on the U.S.!"

He grinned defensively. "Lucretia, my only darling, I love you . . . enormously. But there *are* other things. Other obligations! And my mission!"

Shocked, Lucretia demanded, "What on earth do you mean?"

"The last thing in the world I want is to hurt you," he replied. "I'm so sorry I blurted it out . . . about the mission. Believe me, Lucretia, I love you very much. But I just can't say any more now. Maybe later."

With that curious declaration she had to content herself as best she could. Yet, she was frightened, badly frightened. He would not tell her about those mysterious obstacles to their happiness. He had half-promised to do so, but *when* would that be?

Still shaken, Lucretia later the next evening gazed over the towers of Hong Kong from the balcony of the apartment halfway up the Peak. Pondering long and hard, she asked herself: Do we *really* have a future together, whether in Hong Kong or elsewhere? Or are we too different from each other? What reason is there to believe we can live together happily for many years?

Hong Kong itself was now an issue between them. Robbie was perhaps too comfortable in his little niche. But how long could she bear the cramped life of the enclave?

She already felt hemmed in by the minuscule Colony, oppressed by its teeming millions, and bored by its obsession with business. And life would be even more cramped when the Communists took over! She was fearful of the future Hong Kong. Why else the panic attack and her hesitation to commit herself by sleeping with Robbie, who all but embodied Hong Kong?

Even if Robbie wanted to leave the Colony tomorrow, he could not go for years. His mother was only sixty-four and, aside from her mental deterioration, was in very good health. Even if Robbie had unlimited funds, moving her from the Hong Kong Sanatorium would be extremely difficult, practically impossible. Robbie was further bound to Hong Kong, not only because of his penury but because he was at home here. He was even more strongly bound by his duty to his mother. To an East Asian, filial devotion was far stronger than steel cable.

Trying to look at Robbie objectively, Lucretia saw that he was essentially an East Asian. His cast of mind and his instincts were Asian. That was the trouble. Yet, she acknowledged, his exoticism was also a great attraction. If they were together for fifty years, she'd never be bored by Robbie. He would always surprise her. Yet his alien traits were the root of their differences.

Like herself, Robbie had been read *Dr. Doolittle* and *Winnie the Pooh* when he was very small, even Dr. Seuss. Althea Garland Rabnet had seen to that. They had much more than that essentially Anglo-American upbringing in common. Yet she could not see the rabbit in the moon. He spotted the rabbit easily, but had to look hard to find the man in the moon.

One issue, seemingly superficial, but actually profound, cut to the heart of their relationship. He simply could not give the West credit for what it had built in Asia. He could not acknowledge that foreigners had shaped both Shanghai and Hong Kong. That disagreement was now almost a joke, having been fought out between them so often.

She was also deeply troubled by his lack of candor. The openness that had originally attracted her was now constrained. She was gravely troubled by the mystery he made of his so-called mission. Would he sacrifice himself to his mission and, thus, herself as well? Brooding on that question, she concluded that he would sacrifice them both if necessary.

Central to Robbie's faith was the bodhisattva who rejects Nirvana as long as others remaining outside need his help. That was the ultimate sacrifice a human being could offer, a tribute to universal love of mankind—and all other living beings.

Lucretia asked herself again: Is Robbie, my beloved, not only prepared, but determined to sacrifice himself—and our future—for some abstract ideal? Does he have a bodhisattva complex?

She smiled in self-derision. A bodhisattva complex indeed!

What a ludicrous, irrational term! How could a mix of modish pseudo-Freudian psychobabble and ancient Buddhist lore have any real meaning? It certainly had nothing to do with her Robbie.

BY A JOINT act of will, of which they never spoke, the lovers dispersed the darkness that briefly shadowed their idyll. Both were eager to live to the utmost. Her joy was his, and his joy was hers. The unspoken fear that their time together could be short made their mutual joy especially poignant.

They delighted in the conventional pastimes of conventional lovers. They strolled around the Peak at twilight, holding hands and marveling at the pyrotechnic display below. Outshining the many-colored floodlights that shone on their flanks at dusk, the towers of the city radiated brightness from the windows of thousands of offices where employees and employers toiled together into the night.

Lucretia told Robbie she was working on a big acrylic painting portraying that scene as it had never been portrayed before: from directly above. A myriad of lateral photographs had been taken from the air, but none could capture the panorama that swept from the fishermen's junks in Aberdeen in the south to the towers of Victoria in the north. Only the painter's brush could capture that scene from directly overhead, and only the painter's imagination could impose on it order and logic.

Robbie joked, "It'll look like a big technicolor tank-trap—all spikes and slick concrete."

"Wait and see, my love," Lucretia told him. "It's never been done, so how can you know what it'll look like?

Hong Kong seen from the stratosphere. I may leave out the harbor."

Though shrinking as developers snatched land from the water, Hong Kong harbor seen from the Peak at dusk was a wondrous spectacle. A dozen ferries left luminous tracks like comets' trails among the starry lights of scores of moored ships. Hydrofoils and jetfoils bound for the outer islands or for Macau churned up fizzy white wakes. On the far side of the harbor, innumerable rainbow advertising signs made Kowloon the most gorgeous and the most garish cityscape between Tokyo and Rome.

OLD MRS. SELMA Lotz, whose apartment was across the elevator landing from Lucretia's, loved it when her daughter and her daughter-in-law brought her five grandchildren, all under the age of six. That brood was irrepressibly vivacious, delighting not only their grandmother, but also Lucretia.

All five had bubbled with gleeful anticipation on their last visit. Their mothers had promised to take them teddy bear dancing at the YWCA the next day. Neither mothers nor children had any idea what teddy bear dancing might be. But it sounded terrific.

Lucretia Hatton Barnes, decades older, was also abrim with anticipation. The dawning day, a fine Wednesday in mid-October, would be magical, for Robbie had promised to take her sailing. She'd never been sailing in Hong Kong waters, not really, but had only seen those waters as a passenger on motor-driven vessels of varying splendor. Yet she could not remember when she did not know how to sail. During summers at Martha's Vineyard, she had steered boats ranging from twelve-foot dinghies to a 110-foot schooner.

"This time," Robbie promised, "you'll have a different experience on the water . . . a wholly new sensation."

She rolled her eyes suggestively, and he said with mock severity, "No, not *that!*"

When she pouted extravagantly, he said, "I'll bring Jacobus along—to show that's not, not primarily, what I'm thinking of. You know how he hates it when we're close together."

"He only pretends so he'll get his shinbone. Anyway, he's changed. He now kisses my hand. Very gallant!"

Robbie, the descendant of land-locked Tibetans, but seafaring Britons as well, loved the sea. As a boy, he'd hung around Aberdeen, where foreigners moored their pleasure boats. He was a favorite of the boat-boys, the coxswains who looked after those craft. He did all the tedious chores they disliked: fetching ice, beer, and soft drinks; patching sails; and varnishing woodwork. They in turn introduced him to their owners as a cousin who was learning the trade, and they took him out sailing.

The first large influx of foreigners created a shortage of boat-boys—and Robbie learned to take a boat out alone. Like a caddy picking up golf, he acquired a detailed knowledge of Hong Kong waters, as well as a mariner's certificate, and worked from time to time as a boat-boy. He retired when another large influx of foreigners meant three or four families sharing a single boat—and plaguing their boat-boys with impractical and contradictory instructions. A retired mariner at seventeen, Robbie could always borrow a vessel from the older boat-boys who remembered him fondly.

Robbie, Lucretia, and Jacobus set out for Aberdeen in a taxi on the beautiful morning. A bus would not only have taken longer, but the shih-tzu would not have been welcome.

The vessel was a junk, as were the big broad fishing craft, but a junk with a difference. It was a shrimp boat, long and lean for the speed to get the catch to market first—and command the highest price. Now immaculately maintained as a well-to-do foreigner's plaything, it was called *Hai Shih, Messenger of the Sea.*

Newly varnished teakwood shining in the sunlight, green and red telltales that showed the wind's direction whipping on the wire stays that supported the mast, *Hai Shih* beat out of Aberdeen at half past ten of a lovely morning. Robbie was at the tiller, while Lucretia trimmed the sails.

She laughed in delight as she learned a skill quite different from handling the flexible canvas sails of the Western craft she was used to. The big tan sails resembled the wings of an enormous moth, stiffened as they were by long bamboo battens just as a moth's wings are stiffened by rigid veins. She had to adjust separately each of the seven cords attached to the seven battens that shaped the mainsail to the wind.

When Robbie invited her to take the tiller, Lucretia was surprised at how deftly the rudder, half the size of a barndoor, controlled *Hai Shih.* But she was not so absorbed by the sailing junk as to neglect the unique view of Hong Kong. For the first time she gazed at the island undisturbed by the chatter of other guests on motorized cocktail-lounges. The only sound was the hissing of water along the junk's side and an occasional snore from Jacobus, who'd retired to the mat-roofed cabin for a nap.

Their course skirted the Ocean Park with its performing killer whales and its aerial gondolas whisking visitors overhead on wire cables. They scudded past the Country Club, which shone pearl-white in the sun. Farther along Middle Island with its rows of moored pleasure craft and its pocket golf course divided Deep

Water Bay from Repulse Bay. Above Repulse Bay beach, the pale-yellow colonnaded terrace of the Repulse Bay Hotel fronted the vertical slab of the new building that now housed the guest rooms. At the far end stood the Lifeguard Club, its thirty-foot demigods brilliant in red and blue, its stone menagerie of heavenly animals facing the bay.

Lucretia was fascinated by seeing from the water sights so familiar on land. The shores of Repulse Bay were thick with high-rise buildings piled one on top of the other until they appeared to reach the sky. As seen from the water, they were dwarfed by green hills towering above them, the presumptuous works of men dominated by the enduring works of nature.

"See what I mean?" Robbie asked. "About a different perspective?" He was mesmerized watching her handle the tiller. Her white bikini clinging, without, as she said, "revealing everything." It was modest, practically an enveloping caftan, beside the string bikinis, no more than three triangular scraps of cloth, that were in vogue.

Her tan glowed against the sleek white cloth, and a pale strip on her left wrist showed where she normally wore her watch. Blessedly, her fair skin did not blister under the subtropical sun, but turned pale gold. Her black hair streaming in the wind, she would have made a beautiful figurehead for a rakish schooner.

Passing the Stanley Peninsula, they saw the string of miraculously preserved small elderly houses of Tai Tam Village, overlooked by the high apartment-blocks and the jowl-to-jowl townhouses of Red Hill on the heights across Tai Tam Bay. Lucretia drew in her breath when Robbie pointed to the grim walls of the prison that had been an internment camp for captured civilians in 1942.

"What about lunch?" Lucretia shattered the mood, rather than brood on the inhumanity of that somber sight. "There's champagne—my treat. I sold the picture you said looked like a giant tank-trap. Got a good price, too!"

"You hungry already?"

"I'm just thinking ahead. Women do."

"We'll come about then. The little bay at the top of Lamma Island won't be full of Sunday sailors in the middle of the week."

Robbie steered the junk into the rock-studded anchorage himself. It was not his vessel to risk. He dropped the sails, switched the engine on, and sent Lucretia to the bow to warn of rocks. At his signal, she dropped the anchor, and he allowed *Hai Shih* to drift backward until the pointed flukes took hold on the bottom.

While Robbie let down the wooden swimming ladder, Lucretia found champagne glasses in the picnic basket and a bottle of Pommery in the ice chest. Handing the bottle to him to open, she leaned back against the blue cushions under the sun canopy. He poured the champagne and lifted his glass in salute.

"Just three months today since we met."

"Seems like forever. Also hardly ten minutes ago."

"I thought you were wonderful the first moment I saw you."

"Did you really? I didn't get that impression."

"No, I lie," he confessed. "Interesting, worth further investigation . . . but not wonderful. In actual fact, a little off-putting, bittersweet."

"I guess I was a little stiff . . . cool and defensive," she agreed.

"I thought you were terribly attractive. But I was a little afraid of you . . . of *all* men."

"I'm very glad I persisted. Though I was a bit afraid of you, too."

"I'm glad, too, immensely glad, Robbie. I've never felt like this before. Nothing remotely like this. It's witchcraft . . . magic."

"For me, too."

"You've almost made me believe in magic. . . . Robbie darling, surely you can tell me now. Won't you unravel the mystery of your obligations—and your mission?"

"I'm trying to unravel the obligations, probably can." He rubbed his eyes with his knuckles. "The mission? That word's too grand. It's only a little job of work . . . ongoing work. I'll tell you just as soon as I can . . . I'm allowed to."

She abruptly changed the subject, rather than spoil the day by persisting.

"Oh, dear, I only brought one bikini. I hate sitting around in a wet suit, what there is of it. Robbie, turn around."

"Getting shy in your old age?"

He chuckled, but obediently turned to recork the champagne and replace the bottle in the ice chest.

"Somehow, it's not the same outdoors," she laughed. "Anyway, you can turn back . . . slowly . . . now."

He turned to see her rounded hips and her long slender legs disappear into the green water with hardly a splash. The two white wisps of her bikini lay on the blue cushions.

That smooth dive off the stern, which was ten feet above the water! Lucretia always said her family was poor. But there were poor and poor. From his standpoint, she'd always been privileged. She'd had lessons not only in sailing, but in swimming, diving, tennis, and riding. No more than normal middle-class accomplishments in Cambridge, those skills had been out of his reach in Hong Kong.

Robbie slipped off his trunks and dived from the high stern. When he surfaced after a loud splash, Lucretia called out, "Your world-famous imitation of a sick swan again?"

Jacobus was dancing along the gunwales, barking frantically. He repeatedly placed his front paws on the combing and teetered as if to jump. But he drew back cautiously.

"No swim for you, Jacko," Robbie told him. "I don't want to dry off a wet shih-tzu today. Too much like work."

"Oh, let him come in," Lucretia pleaded. "I'll wash out the salt when we get back."

"You heard the lady, Jacko," Robbie said resignedly. "Come on in."

Jacobus hurled himself head first into the water, his long ears streaming. After a mighty splash, he paddled happily in circles, not venturing far from the boat. Raising his head, he barked joyfully in a forced falsetto.

Robbie climbed the short wooden ladder, calling over his shoulder, "You notice I'm not asking you to turn around."

"Don't be so vain, my boy. It's not bad, but I've seen dozens better."

"The devil you have!"

Clinging to the ladder with one hand, Lucretia caught Jacobus around the middle and handed him to Robbie. She climbed the ladder and stood dripping on the deck.

This time, Robbie did not look away but happily watched her appear from the sea like the Botticelli painting she called "Aphrodite on the Half Shell."

Drops of water sparkled like chip diamonds on Lucretia's breasts and hips. The dark delta between her thighs shimmered with tiny droplets. No longer shy, or self-conscious, she stepped into his arms.

Silent for once, Jacobus looked on with great interest, his head cocked to one side. After a minute or so, he was satisfied that they meant each other no harm. Bored with the display of flashing legs and twisting torsos, he retreated to the cabin for another nap.

Later, they ate the celebratory lunch she had packed: paté de foie gras, giant prawns in homemade mayonnaise, and a salad of green arugula, rosy radicchio, and white mozzarella cheese garnished with fresh basil leaves. They sipped the champagne and later slept for an hour or so, waking to make love again slowly and lazily.

The enchanted day ended with a theatrical sunset. Incandescent pink, violet, and gold streaks gleamed above the moth-wing sails of the junk silhouetted against the bright horizon to the west.

9

"THEY'RE NOT HERE because it's picturesque," Robbie snapped. "They're here because it's cheap."

Lucretia could no longer count on his ever even temper, not after his explosion at the Chung Yeung party. Still, he had been provoked, this flash of irritation while they ate crisp noodles garnished with shredded crab was her own fault. She had been gushing about the picturesque setting where workers and clerks congregated in the evening. When it came to the poor of the Colony, Robbie tended to lose his normal cool British detachment. Somehow, he felt an obligation toward those who had not notably profited from the rolling Hong Kong boom of the past few decades.

That reaction, Lucretia reflected again, must spring from his bodhisattva complex, his sense of responsibility for those less fortunate than himself. She had to accept this complex as a fact of life, however difficult it could prove in the future, however awkward that term itself.

Robbie believed he could not enjoy true happiness unless he helped the impoverished, the maimed, and the exploited, giving his time to them and the few dollars he could. If that was not a neurotic complex, what was? It was like a bodhisattva's sacrificing immediate joy by refusing to enter Nirvana, the Buddhist Heaven, until all living beings had done so—"down to the last blade of grass," as the homily said.

His overreaching compassion and his readiness, almost eagerness, to make sacrifices for others had been learned from his religious instructors. But those traits were now ingrained, all but automatic. Lucretia could only hope she herself would not be sacrificed—nor their future.

She dismissed her fears and looked around appreciatively. No matter how Robbie saw it, the evening scene was picturesque—both spectacular and touchingly human. She was itching to paint it.

Robbie's love and admiration had brought her alive again. She lived, however, most intensely when she had a brush in her hand. He had taught her to be confident in being herself again, and she was, she realized anew, for better or for worse an artist. She rose eagerly to the challenge of depicting the night market's brilliant glare and its midnight black shadows. Between bites, she was roughing details into the sketchbook she always carried with her nowadays.

It was called *Dai Pai Dong,* loosely translated as the Grand Treasurehound of Quality Goods, though it was really an acre or so of open-air stalls. The Dai Pai Dong on Jordon Road in Kowloon was not yet sanitized and denatured, as were its counterparts elsewhere. It had not yet been rendered commonplace and sterile by electricity that elsewhere fed street lights and big white refrigerators. Still lit primarily by big gas lamps, it was the shopping mall of the poor. Though of course, Lucretia reflected, most of the poor of Hong Kong were bloated plutocrats beside the poor of Africa or India.

Giant acetylene lanterns hissing like snakes cast jagged blue-white light over the food stalls and the long board counters set on sawhorses. Those boards were spread with cheap merchandise ranging from plastic household implements to flashy T-shirts bearing meaningless mottos in what was supposed to be English. The sharp alteration of light and shadow, the shadowed faces, and the half-glimpsed dramas among the ramshackle booths made a riveting tableau. The Cantonese patrons were always theatrical, and the night market itself was enchanted, vanishing with the daylight. Besides, this Dai Pai Dong served the best noodles in the Colony.

Lucretia saw from the shadow on Robbie's face that he was again brooding on the issue that had preoccupied him for more than a week. Yet to her that issue was reasonably straightforward—and the solution was obvious.

"If I do go along," he said abruptly, "they'll think I caved in under pressure—the threats and the promises. Everyone'll think I've been bribed."

"Worse things could happen!" she replied shortly.

"What do you mean?"

"A little credit with the new bosses won't do you any harm. The future's roaring down on us. Only a few months till the People's Liberation Army marches in, starched and polished for the occasion. Since you're determined to stay, you—we—can use all the goodwill we can get."

"You say *we!*" He paused. "Does that mean what I think? You'll stay with me?"

"I'll try hard to . . . if they let me. I haven't exactly cultivated their goodwill, have I? . . Oh, Robbie, did you really think I'd desert you?"

"This is the first time you've promised outright. I'm very glad!"

He had, she thought, turned her promise to try to stay into a commitment to do so. But she did not protest. This was no time to split hairs.

"It's not just bloody-mindedness, you know," he resumed. "Nor because I like the Communists. It's for Hong Kong, for my hometown, as you Yanks say. Frankly, I *want* to stay. Besides, I've *got* to."

"I know, Robbie. Your mother, of course. And what else? Why do you protest so much?"

At a disadvantage, Robbie stammered, "Because . . . because you don't really believe me."

"Of course I do." Feeling his discomfort, she turned the conversation, "What're you going to do about those girders?"

"I haven't quite decided."

"I know, dear, it's easy for me to give advice, to push you in one direction. Sure, my fate's tied to yours, but I'm still an outsider. And I'm not bound by professional scruples. Anyway, why not go over the pros and cons again?"

"All right. First, the basic issue's really a formality. The steel girders in H. K. Lam's latest architectural atrocity are only millimeters short of specifications. Hong Kong standards, you know, are always excessive—to make up for the universal cheating. By any other standard, the girders're adequate, if only just. There's no danger to life or property."

"Then why not, for God's sake, just certify them?"

"Because they are *not* up to Hong Kong standards. Because I've got a professional conscience. Because it's a lie . . ."

"Only a *white* lie."

"But still a lie. And what if they *don't* hold?"

"They will. My favorite expert says so. . . . Suppose you don't go along, Robbie? Suppose you blow the whistle. What then?"

"Lam'll get an exception, sure as shooting. He'll bring in a carload of experts, but it's a foregone conclusion. I'll be over-ruled, ticked off for excessive zeal. Nit-picking, in other words."

His grin belied his serious meaning, and he added, "Regardless, building'll proceed. And H. K. Lam, that model of respectability—and opportunism—will be forgiven after handing out some tea money. He's so well in with the Beijing crowd, he mightn't need to bother with tea money. Regardless, he'll be forgiven—and he'll be told to carry on."

"So it won't make any difference whatever you do. Then what's the holdup? Why don't you just certify it, get it over with?"

"Because I *do* have professional scruples. They want a clean bill of health, not just a waiver of a minor technical insufficiency. The motherland lovers, the Chinese bastards with their billions and their new so-called patriotic support for the Communists. I don't want them to think I'm an easy mark. Otherwise, how could I go on working?"

"You won't be working at all if you rub them the wrong way." She reached across the rickety table and laid her hand on his. "My dear, please do it for me."

"But it's the thin edge of the wedge . . . the camel's getting his nose under the tent." He grinned at the mixed metaphors, and she capped them: "Not to speak of letting the lead sled dog sleep in the igloo."

"All right! I'll go along. Let them think I'm an easy mark. Let them hold me in contempt and—"

"It's really my fault," Lucretia interrupted. "It's on my shoulders—pressing you to go against your conscience."

"The final responsibility's mine. Though really I've got no choice. I've got to stay in Hong Kong . . . not only because of Mum."

"What else is there?"

He hesitated, then leaned toward her and spoke in a low voice, "Tibet needs a man here, a man who can travel in China. The Dalai Lama has to know what's going on. I seem to be that man. Now you won't mention . . ."

So that was it. Finally, he'd given her a hint about his mission.

"For God's sake, Robbie," she protested, "do you think I'd pass on anything you told me?"

Lucretia did not press him, knowing she would learn more when he wished to tell her. But she wondered about her own motives. Why was she urging Robbie to leave the door open and not make it impossible for him to work in Hong Kong after June 30 of next year? Why was she advising him to compromise with the henchmen of the incoming Beijing regime? Did she not in the depths of her heart want both of them to be gone when the Communists took over?

Or did she really?

Her purposes, she realized, were badly confused. She really wanted to be gone before the Communists arrived. Yet she wanted above all to be with Robbie.

Amid her perplexity, Lucretia suddenly saw the apparently ordinary yet striking picture that she wanted to paint. It was quintessentially Hong Kong.

A tarpaulin slung on bamboo poles protected the several flimsy glass-and-wood foodstalls from the light rain. The dry area amid the mirror gleam of wet pavement was lit by the yellow glow of kerosene lanterns, rather than the harsh blue-white glare of acetylene. Spotlighted by a freak beam of brightness, a middle-aged worker wearing a crumpled blue cotton jacket over a soiled undershirt was perched on a flimsy folding chair at a wobbly round table. One horny foot was cocked on a small bamboo stool, a green plastic sandal dangling from his toes.

Oblivious to all else, his gaze was fixed on the blue-and-white rice bowl in his left hand. His bamboo chopsticks shoveled into his mouth garish orange tidbits made from unidentifiable parts of pigs' innards. He looked like an unmovable rock.

She would call the painting *The Survivor*.

THE LOVERS DID not gloat on the joys of their future together. They were afraid to jinx their happiness by talking about it too much—by hoping too much, even by believing too much. Only fools offended fate by flaunting their joy.

Robbie was rigorously logical, as became a practical engineer. His Buddhism required arduous mental effort, as well as sheer devotion. It was no simple faith for old ladies, hardly a matter of burning a few sticks of incense to please the gods or predicting the future by the marking on slips of wood picked at random from a vase by a tame bird.

Lucretia was an agnostic. She was not convinced of the existence of a single deity, much less a multitude. She prided herself upon her rationality, but she had lived too long in Hong Kong not to be infected by its universal superstition.

The super-rich, whom she knew so well, were even more gullible than the masses to omens and portents. They strove to manipulate the future by flattering and bribing the myriad gods and goddesses: Confucian, Taoist, Buddhist, and Christian, too. The super-rich could afford whatever it took to wheedle from the gods fulfillment of the four greatest human cravings: health, happiness, longevity, and, however ironically, even more wealth.

Despite their subliminal fear of jinxing their future by dwelling on it, the lovers naturally discussed the bitter question of Hong Kong's prospects after June 30, 1997. Yet Robbie was still rather cagey, for his reticence had become a habit. And Lucretia was still learning more about the grisly details of Communist rule in China. But she already knew enough to be fearful of Beijing's rule in Hong Kong, though she no longer pressed Robbie to put their future before his mission. So they did not talk much about their own future in Hong Kong.

Separately, however, each thought long and hard about that future. Separately, each assumed that their life together would fit his or her vision. Yet their individual visions diverged.

She could not imagine living indefinitely under a harsh authoritarian regime that swayed the people by crude Chinese nationalism. He could not imagine leaving Hong Kong, his home, no matter who ruled it. Both based their hopes on unspoken assumptions, rather than shared judgments. Neither would have bought a car—*if* they could ever afford a car—without talking it over with the other. Yet they were moving towards the most crucial decision of their lives without really consulting each other.

FOR HONG KONG ostentation and extravagance, it was hard to beat the stratospherically expensive restaurant called Kuang Xi, literally Manic Joy, and, thus by logical extension, Ecstasy.

The lovers could not even think of eating at that restaurant on their own—not now, not ever. When Robbie was invited to a dinner at the Kuang Xi by a client, Lucretia and he approached the hammered brass doors through rows of Rolls-Royces with nattily uniformed chauffeurs.

Their billionaire host was celebrating the sale of his latest office tower. Though it was still incomplete, he'd already turned a profit of seven hundred percent on his original investment, which had been provided at low interest by the Hong Kong & Shanghai Bank. Although an unreformed capitalist, a speculator, and a predator, he stood high in Beijing's favor, since he endorsed whatever the Communists wanted in the Colony. The largest British bank was therefore currying favor with him, as it was with all the super-rich, newly leftist opportunists.

The invitation had been formal and flowery: gold Chinese characters embossed on red silk. It was, however, understood that the billionaires and the mere multimillionaires would not bring their wives. Robbie had, nonetheless, brought Lucretia. As a wife, she had never attended such a stag dinner Hong Kong style. As a mistress, she was, however, welcome.

Robbie still had some misgivings about her presence. He was proud of Lucretia and jealous of her good name. Yet he had never thought of marrying her. That aspect of his future was already preempted by two Tibetan women. He was being pressed to marry one woman by his grandmother in Lhasa, the other by the Hong Kong Old Lama. As he wondered uneasily whether he should have brought her to this dinner, his thoughts turned to marriage with Lucretia—and he realized that he had no intention of ever marrying her. The notion was very attractive in the abstract: spending the rest of his life with her. But he could not even consider marrying her. The prior claims on him and his devotion to his Tibetan roots both made it impossible.

Robbie would not have brought Lucretia if she had not insisted on seeing this new side of Hong Kong. He would certainly not have brought her if he had not been confident that nothing unseemly would occur. The dinner party would be decorous, though hardly staid. Yet everyone was already drinking too much, even himself, who normally stuck to beer and not that much beer. He gulped when he saw the women brought by other guests.

Lulu Wong, the most notorious and most costly courtesan in the Colony, wore an ankle-length cheongsam of shimmering gold cloth slit high to display garters set with semiprecious stones clustered around big black pearls. She flaunted a five-karat blue-white diamond pendant on a necklace that was itself almost as valuable: three strands of graduated sea-green jade beads confected in the Ming Dynasty.

Less serene and less ladylike than the queenly Lulu, the other women were vivid splashes of color among the men's dark suits, even more flamboyantly clad than she and almost as flamboyantly begemmed. The rich of Hong Kong had once paraded their wealth by their wives' jewelry, minks, and sables. But their ostentation had never been as lavish or as gaudy as the new super-rich's display of wealth beyond counting on the persons of their concubines and girlfriends.

Lucretia must feel outshone, even dowdy, in her severely cut suit of heavy midnight-blue tribute silk, Robbie reflected ruefully. Her only jewelry was her mother's old-fashioned sunburst brooch. Yet in his eyes Lucretia's elegant simplicity made Lulu look tawdry.

Despite his misgivings at her mixing with such women, Lucretia had argued, "Chinese men hardly think of a Western female as a woman, much less a sex object. They never think of *any* woman as a partner. Even . . . no, especially, the comrades in Beijing. They *know* all women are inferior."

Western women, Robbie had agreed, were repugnant to most Chinese men for their pallid complexions, their assertiveness, and the peculiar odor their coarse skin gave to perfumes that were seductive on Chinese women. He suspected that rich Chinese men were slightly repelled by the Australian, European, and American tarts they paraded on their arms. They were, however, perversely fascinated by blondes and redheads. Unlike the indentured Caucasian taxi dancers, most of them Russians, in the secret society-dominated public ballrooms of Macau and Hong Kong, this flashy foreign sisterhood were valued primarily as showy trophies. Unlike the taxi dancers, who knew they would be murdered if they broke their contracts with the Russian Mafia, these women of pleasure were freelancers. They were also very costly.

Fortunately, no foreign trollops were present tonight. And everyone knew that Dorje Rabnet could not afford a taxi dancer for an evening, much less a full-time mistress. It had to be love. And that the assembled Chinese tycoons considered very peculiar. But what could you expect of one who was doubly a barbarian—half Tibetan and half English?

Under the eyes of their mistresses and girlfriends, the host and his guests flirted outrageously with the waitresses, who wore skimpy parodies of dinner jackets with skin-tight black slacks.

They flirted even more broadly with the five hostesses, whose gold-bordered cheongsams, snug across unrestrained breasts, were slit even higher than Lulu Wong's. Male hands groped scandalously—to be rebuffed by demonstrative mock female slaps and shrill forced female laughter. Fortunately, the raw jokes in raucous Cantonese or sibilant Shanghainese were meaningless to Lucretia. Nonetheless, her smile was strained.

Between the gold-toned mirrors on the walls hung traditional paintings of scenes at the last Imperial Court. Clearly very expensive, those scrolls drew sharp intakes of breath from the super-rich. Their hearts were moved, above all, by large sums. Tonight they were moved as well by rediscovered Chinese nationalism, their regenerated Chinese hearts delighted by the splendors of the non-Chinese Manchu Dynasty.

Jade flowerpots set on antique rosewood altar tables held bouquets of jade, garnet, turquoise, and alabaster blossoms. Spotlights inset in scarlet, emerald, and gold ceilings, where dragons and phoenixes romped, lit giant bronze and yellow chrysanthemums in enormous porcelain vases made for emperors.

Robbie glanced at the the leather-bound menu, which was as thick as a Bible, and whistled at the prices and the curious English beneath the Chinese descriptions. A small bowl of "Double Boiled Shark's Fins with Tsicken and Yunnan Ham" went for HK$300, about US$40, and "Five Kynds of Snake in Superior Broth Served with Chrysanthemum Petals" for more than US$200. "Double Boiled Deer Penis with Tsicken and Chinese Herbs" at HK$2,000 was not to be served tonight, rather unfortunately. Many of the aging plutocrats present surely needed that aid to virility. Of course, the Cantonese considered most foods a treatment as well as a treat—and many foods surefire aphrodisiacs.

Robbie did some quick mental arithmetic. Even without the deer penises, this banquet could hardly cost less than US$2,000 a head—and there were sixty guests at the five round tables. Now US$120,000 was a good round sum.

Robbie had feared that Lucretia's austere New England standards would make her uneasy amid the showy luxury. But she was not visibly repelled by the jamboree of bad taste. No more was she dazzled. In fact, she rather enjoyed the spectacle she watched under modestly downcast eyelids. She was disgusted at being in the same room as H. K. Lam, who had baited her at the architect's dinner. She was, however, not particularly shocked by the antics of the super-rich when they left their wives behind.

Robbie's protector, the banker T. Y. Lee, charmed her. Robbie had not told her of the banker's warning him off her. Why hurt her by recalling the old man's advice that he could be badly injured professionally, even destroyed, by associating with a woman who was self-exiled from Hong Kong's gilded society, who was an outspoken foe of the incoming Communist regime?

During the predinner drinks, Beijing's lackey H. K. Lam was too busy to renew his attack. He was receiving congratulations on behalf of their host—and for himself, as well.

As the billionaire's senior legal adviser, H. K. Lam, Queen's Counsel, was jackal-in-chief to one of the fifty richest men in the world. No task was so great as to awe him; no task was so sordid as to sicken him. Like the vizier of a powerful sultan, his chief concern was to serve his master diligently. His secondmost concern was to avoid appearing more powerful than the sultan himself.

His reward was not the crumbs from his master's table, but ducks' tongues, sharks' fins, bears' paws, and swallows' nests—all the exotic and costly delicacies wealthy Chinese consumed with ostentatious pleasure. Also the vintage champagnes, the US$2,000-a-bottle Bordeaux and Burgundies, the pearly heaps of fresh caviar, and the shimmering white truffles the super-rich had learned to relish from their foreign associates.

H. K. Lam was even allowed to build for himself. He could not keep from cheating a little—as he had on the short steel girders that were giving Robbie such heartache. Above all, he was attentive to Beijing's commands. His subservience had won him a senior position on Beijing's rubber-stamp Preparatory Council for the transfer of Hong Kong. H. K. Lam was one of a few hundred selected to preside in name over the transformation of relatively free Hong Kong into a puppet of Beijing.

Lam looked even more like an overfed bullfrog than he had a few months earlier. Behind the enormous round spectacles that magnified his bulging eyes, his fleshy face was a sickly pale green from too many banquets, too much self-indulgence, and almost no exercise. His obesity was imperfectly camouflaged by the double-breasted dinner jacket that strained across his mountainous paunch.

He had not resumed his attack on Lucretia just now when they met again. He was far too well trained to spoil his master's victory party. He had, however, allowed himself a grimace of disbelief, his slack lips parted in demonstrative astonishment at her presence.

"So you've seen the light, Mrs. Barnes?" he boomed. "Joined us to ride the wave of the future? Very sensible!"

Lucretia only smiled and replied vaguely, "Something like that!"

She was already turning away but Lam persisted, "I'm glad

there's no more nonsense about art in buildings. To get along in Hong Kong, you must compromise, give and take."

She would have to tell Robbie that Lam was aware of his unhappiness over the skimped girders. But she replied noncommittally, "I guess so. Now, if you'll excuse me . . ."

Feeling Robbie's hand on her arm, she turned away. He led her to an easy chair that sheltered a frail figure who looked too small for his worn shawl-collared dinner jacket.

"Uncle, may I present Lucretia Hatton Barnes?" Robbie hated calling her *Mrs.* Barnes. "Lucretia, this is my mother's old friend T. Y. Lee, the wisest man in Hong Kong. No, not just Hong Kong. The wisest man in Asia."

"You might as well say the wisest man in the world, and have done with it," the old man chided. "Pay no heed to Dorje's nonsense, Mrs. Barnes. I just keep an ear to the ground. And I've been lucky, very lucky. That's my only secret."

"And you're sharing it with us," she smiled. "How generous!"

"I regret that I can only share the secret. Sadly, I cannot give you a piece of my luck. Nothing would please me more."

"And your wisdom?"

"Not wisdom, my dear, just experience. Only a fool could live for eighty-five years—and not learn something of the ways of the world."

T. Y. Lee's small eyes sparkled in their webs of crow's feet, and he gestured widely with his translucent, liver-spotted hand. His thready voice fell, and Lucretia leaned closer to hear the words spoken in a mellow Cambridge accent.

"You know, my dear, I advised Dorje to avoid you at all costs." He smiled when she shook her head in disbelief.

"What, he never told you? Wise fellow. Seeing you now, talking with you, I know I was wrong. You're so attractive no man in his right mind could stay away from you. And, I'm told, brainy, too."

"Please don't flatter me, Mr. Lee. I'm no more than—"

"You're quite right about Beijing's rule of Hong Kong." His voice dropped even lower, and she strained to hear him. "An unmitigated disaster. Anyone who can is well advised to leave. I myself . . . But I talk too much. My dear, you mustn't tell anyone but Dorje what I've said. I'm not quite ready to go public."

"As if I would, Mr. Lee!"

"You must call me Uncle as Dorje does. Mr. Lee is so formal."

Lucretia realized that she was flirting with the invincibly charming octogenarian. She smiled, touched his hand, and said, "I do hope we'll meet again . . . Uncle Lee."

"Certainly we will. I'll see to that. Good-bye for now, my dear."

When they found their place cards, Lucretia was seated beside Robbie in the forthright Chinese manner. Why bring your woman to a banquet and then sit at separate tables or far apart at the same table? They were directly across from Lulu Wong, who was H. K. Lam's date, if such an innocent description could apply to such an overpowering professional beauty. On Lulu Wong's left sat T. Y. Lee.

Seeing them together, H. K. Lam chatting with Lulu Wong and T. Y. Lee smiling benignly, their joint nickname, Tweedlelam and Tweedlelee, was hard to understand. They were not at all alike: Cambridge versus Oxford; slight versus corpulent; witty versus ponderous; gentle mannered versus overbearing; quick-witted versus obtuse; and, from what Robbie said, scrupulously honest, at least for free-wheeling Hong Kong, versus foully corrupt, even for nefarious Hong Kong.

The silent enmity between the two snapped in that instant. Evidently reacting to some inane remark H. K. Lam had just made to Lulu Wong, perhaps a promise of even greater privileges after June 1997, old T. Y. Lee suggested conversationally, "Old friend Lam, do try not to be even more stupid than God made you! Do you truly believe you'll cut a grand figure when our Crown Colony of Hong Kong becomes their Special Administrative Region? Do you truly believe the commissars will allow you—or the toady they're making Chief Executive—any freedom of maneuver, much less independent authority?"

"Why the devil do you think they asked me to co-chair the Preparatory Council?" H. K. Lam's indignant rumble drew the gaze of all at the table. "Just for the devil of it?"

"They asked me, too," the old banker replied softly. "But I declined."

"The more fool you," the lawyer exploded. "Missing the chance to get in on the ground floor. Spurning the opportunity to serve the motherland—and be liberally rewarded."

"You got in on the ground floor—and you'll stay there. It's all a sham. Why does Beijing scorn even the limited democracy London finally gave us? Only because they require total control. Also to keep the infection spreading to the Mainland. Can't you grasp the simple truth? They're predators, not collaborators with free enterprise.

"My dear old Lam, I'll tell you again: He who lives by greed perishes by greed."

The entire table was listening intently. The lawyer's bellowed responses to the banker's soft-voiced jabs also attracted stares from neighboring tables. But T. Y. Lee and H. K. Lam went at each other as if they were closeted in private. The mutual contempt, the rivalry and the enmity of decades were spilling out like torrents from a burst dam.

"Do you truly believe you can bribe the big guns in Beijing the way you've bribed your people here?" T. Y. Lee's thready voice conveyed incredulity, amusement, and scorn. "Even though your various masters've contributed hundreds of millions—no, maybe billions—for monuments projects in China . . . and've bribed senior generals and politicos lavishly, they'll nonetheless take whatever they fancy. You're only bidding up the price of serfdom, paying well over the odds for the privilege of giving up your freedom.

"Worse practically, you and your partners are in league with antagonistic factions in Beijing. The President and the Premier are striving to expand their individual power, while the Liberation Army holds the decisive cards. And the President's gang wants to replace Hong Kong with Shanghai as the financial center of East Asia. What a stinking kettle of fish!"

Although H. K. Lam was now purple with outrage, he replied condescendingly, "Lee, I've said it before, and I'll say it again. You're simply a subversive, always against authority. Where's your patriotism, your love for the motherland?"

"*Your* motherland, Lam, not mine. And when was your fervid patriotism born? You ran away from Mao Zedong's Red Guards who were meant to pour across the border in sixty-seven. Ran away for 'medical treatment,' reckoning it'd be healthier for you far away. And you said flatly that you hated Communist influence in the Colony, . . said it would be death to free enterprise.

"Do you really think they've changed just because they let you pour billions into useless real estate in Shanghai? Just because they've appointed four hundred stooges to choose the new Chief Executive? That's their answer to the people's demand for democracy—a rigged committee.

"You know, Governor Chris Patten's a good chap—and not just for a politician; he's made a big contribution: taught the people of Hong Kong there's an alternative to despots—and frightened the despot's democracy would spread inland. Of course no institutions could keep the commissars in line. Certainly not creating a Hong Kong Chinese civil service so the Communists wouldn't remodel it? Nonsense! They always do as they please. Promises and treaties be damned.

"They're still the same old gang: murderers, thieves, and extortionists. You and your lot're their eager henchmen, the murderers' accomplices."

"Just wait, you old fool," H. K. Lam sputtered. "Wait and see what happens to you when they come. It's already happening to your half-caste Tibetan protégé and his harridan of a racist anti-Chinese Yankee girlfriend. Is he too dense to see that his work is falling off—and will fall a lot more?"

Lucretia turned to Robbie and saw, beneath his noncommittal expression that it was true. She smiled fleetingly at Robbie, deliberately showing neither surprise nor concern. Robbie's wry smile in return sealed the immediate unspoken pledge between them.

He had no need of words to say: I'll always stick with you, even if there's no work at all. But there will be.

Nor did she need spoken words to tell him: Of course, there'll be work. They're not all powerful. But if you feel trapped . . . deadly pressed . . . I'll let you go.

It won't happen. It'll never come to that! he replied, and their silent dialogue was concluded.

At the same time, T. Y. Lee said to Lam, "More fool you, to deprive yourself of the best counsel you can get, the professional judgment of Dorje Rabnet!

"Myself, I'm much too old to worry. They can only kill me or jail me. So I'll hang on as long as I can. I want to see with my own eyes what happens to scum like you when you're no longer useful—when the commissars have squeezed you dry."

The two old men seethed. They had before this evening been restrained in public by Confucian etiquette and the code of the English gentleman who never shows emotion. They were now haranguing each other like drunken coolies.

"Lee, I'll see you hanged—after you're stripped of everything you own."

"What I haven't squirreled away abroad. By the way, Lam, how many hundred millions've you siphoned into Canada and Switzerland?"

"Not a penny!" Realizing his denial was not believable, Lam clamped his slack lips together and took on a new tack: "Trouble with you, Lee, is you can't change, not ever. You can't adjust to the new reality."

Lam smiled benevolently and continued in an unctuous tone, "I and my colleagues and friends, we'll look after the poor who can't leave. There'll be freedom to speak out, to write, as long as it doesn't undermine the government in Hong Kong or in Beijing. And, as long as we can do business—and that'll be a long, long time—we'll look after men and women like my friends Mr. and Mrs. Sha. They run a small shop in the Pedder Building selling hand embroidery—old-fashioned embroidery that's out of fashion today. They pay Hong Kong five thousand a month in rent—and that's hard to scrape up. So much for the kindly British government.

"Their sons don't look after them. The family system's been razed by go-ahead Hong Kong. But we'll look after them. They'll be far better off under a compassionate socialist government. And no one will interfere with our freely doing business."

"So you'll forget about free culture, all the grace notes: painting, the theater, music, poetry, even journalism. Even so, do you really believe the commissars'll let you get away with your old tricks?" Lam's tormentor retorted softly. "They want all the loot themselves. No more middlemen. You won't be able to build ten times as many stories as your permit specifies. Or put a little more sand in the foundations, less steel in the girders. Or your latest trick, sweeping away the Hong Kong Sanatorium to build a new tower for block offices. Is that your compassion?"

"Everything you touch turns to dung, Lee. Honest patriots can't stand you. You're a turd from a corpse, a running dog for the lousy British. You're a pile of stinking dog droppings!"

T. Y. Lee did not reply. He only smiled as if to say, There it is, ladies and gentlemen. The rascal is beyond rational discourse. He can only bluster and swear.

Icy calm, T. Y. Lee addressed himself to the food. That gesture was the ultimate expression of his scorn for H. K. Lam and their host. He could as well have said aloud that he considered them contemptible, unworthy of normal courtesies. He would, therefore, not walk out of the banquet, as he would had they been honorable antagonists. Neither they nor their food was worth spurning.

. . .

WHEN THE HOST finally rose to signal that the banquet was at an end, the guests poured out of the fantasy world of the restaurant. Robbie and Lucretia found themselves beside T. Y. Lee.

"I'm sorry you had to put up with that, my dears," he said. "It's been boiling for decades—and it finally erupted. I thoroughly enjoyed my little discussion with the jackal, though I fear it offended some. . . . Dorje, I'm afraid it's true about the Hong Kong Sanatorium. We'll have to see about Althea."

"And *you* warned *me* to be careful!" Robbie's words were slightly slurred—by astonishment as well as by the brandy and *mao tai* he had consumed in unaccustomed profusion.

"I did, didn't I?" the irrepressible banker replied. "I've already said I was wrong about your Lucretia—apologized to her. Still, I won't offer you a lift. Too shaming to ride with the pariah."

The old man's ancient chauffeur solicitously helped him into the fire-engine-red Rolls-Royce. It drew away before the rest of the limousines, while the other guests watched in lingering astonishment at T. Y. Lee's battle with H. K. Lam.

Robbie's voice was charged with awe and wonder, "And he told me to watch *my* step! The face they lost, Lam and our host! Immense!"

He turned to Lucretia and said low-voiced, enunciating painstakingly to avoid slurring his words, "I've been hinting. Meant to tell you earlier, should've told you outright days ago. I'm taking off day after tomorrow, going to see the Dalai Lama in India at his command. Then to Tibet, all the way to Lhasa. I don't want to go, hate leaving you even for a few weeks. But there's no help for it. My grandmother, too. The old girl absolutely insists!"

10

EARLY THE NEXT morning, Lucretia awoke to a nagging head-ache—and knew she was in the grip of a slight hangover. The sensation was unfamiliar since she, like Robbie, was normally a moderate drinker. She could just imagine how he would feel awakening alone in his tiny apartment. As well as Scotch and brandy, he had drunk three thimble-cups of fierce mao tai to her one.

The medicated spirits in the white-glass bottle that pretended to be porcelain were favored for Chinese celebrations. God alone knew why! Mao tai reeked like a medieval alchemist's laboratory with acrid, sour, and putrid stenches. It tasted like kerosene laced with chlorine—and just a cup or two made the morning after painful.

Poor Robbie! Poor Robbie indeed! Damn Robbie!

Tightlipped, she had turned down his invitation to his cramped flat. And she had conspicuously failed to invite him to her new place. For the first time since she'd known him, he was the worse for drink. What really hurt, she recalled with renewed indignation, was his waiting till the end of the trying evening to spring on her the fact that he was leaving for Tibet in a day or two.

She recalled his slurred confession with pained precision. Like any devout Tibetan making for the motherland, he would stop at the Dalai Lama's hill-town refuge in northern India. And he would be received in private audience by the legitimate spiritual and temporal ruler of Tibet. On the road to Lhasa, Robbie had hinted, he would confer with leaders of the continuing resistance to Chinese rule, the cause for which his father had died.

Still, there was nothing sinister, no cloak and dagger hocus-pocus about Robbie's obeying his grandmother's summons to Lhasa. At least that purpose of his journey was not clothed with mystery. Yet it still rankled. Why hadn't he told her earlier, but only when he'd had too much to drink? And precisely what did his grandmother want of him?

Well, she only had to ask. And why not right now? It was just past seven, but he was an early riser.

Yet Lucretia hesitated. Asian men complained about the assertiveness of foreign women, particularly American women. Acceptable behavior varied sharply from East to West. In some respects, Robbie was wholly Asian. The last thing she wanted was to badger him, make him think her a shrew.

Though he usually left for work by eight, he would leave even earlier today if a hangover kept him from sleeping. Lucretia dialed Robbie's eight-digit number. He answered so promptly he must have been hovering over the telephone.

"Good morning, Robbie," she said. "I hope your head doesn't ache like mine."

"Poor darling," he said. "I'll bet mine's worse. I always swear I'll stay away from the mao tai—and then guzzle it. China's secret weapon against all foreigners."

"How much do you remember about last night?" she asked in a neutral tone.

"A fair bit. The battle royal between Tweedlelee and Tweedlelam, who could forget it? The grapevines'll be humming all over town. I could dine out on it for weeks."

"What else do you remember?"

"There was something about . . . Damnation! Did old Lee say something about the Hong Kong Sanatorium closing down?"

"He said H. K. Lam and his fellow bandits were closing it so they could build on the site. He also said he'd see that your mother was all right."

"Easy for him to say. Any change is bound to upset her badly. And the cost! There's nothing else for her except the MacLehose Clinic—and that costs a bomb."

"He hinted that he'd look after it."

"Thank God! If the old man said that, he'll see her right. But she'll hate being trundled from place to place."

"No need to worry till it actually happens. Robbie, what else do you remember?"

"Is this some kind of memory test?"

"I'd just like to hear more about something you said."

"What's that?"

"You told me you were going to Tibet. Don't you remember?"

"Did I say that? How extraordinary! What could've got into me to say a thing like that?"

Lucretia laughed and said lightly, "Please don't keep me in the dark like a mushroom and pile lies on me."

"So you really believe you heard me say I was going to Tibet?"

"Definitely! Also something about your grandmother's summoning you."

"Now I see it, love. The old girl's always sending urgent messages, demanding I come to Lhasa to see her. I had another not so long ago. It's routine, nothing to get excited about."

Although she was pressing his fraying patience, Lucretia did not retreat. His evasions were angering her.

"It didn't seem routine last night, Robbie. Please stop dodging and tell me about your going to Lhasa."

"I really said that! Any rate, you *think* you heard me say it. Now that *is* remarkable. How could I have . . ."

Very gently, Lucretia returned the headset to its cradle. Though she hated to hang up on Robbie, she would explode if she listened to his feeble evasions any longer. She knew she had not misunderstood him, and she would certainly not call him again. Old-fashioned or not, it was now up to him to call her.

Of course, she'd never hesitated to call when she wanted to see him. But this was different. Did she really want to see him just now and provoke a confrontation? No, she would not play emotional roulette with the stake the most interesting man she had ever met, the man whom she loved deeply. She decided to do nothing.

Two days passed, then three, four, five—and Robbie still did not call. Lucretia knew she should not have hung up on him. Better to have had it out right then.

• • •

ON THE EVENING of the sixth day, Lucretia and Robbie were both working late at their offices, his in Central, hers at the Chinese University in the New Territories. It was past eight when each picked up a telephone at almost the same moment and dialed the other's familiar home number—and reached an answering machine. When she returned after midnight, Lucretia heard Robbie's message: "Now I know why people say they can't live without someone else. I always thought that was pure bilge, but I'm not so sure now. Lucretia, I'm dying to see you. Can I come round tomorrow night? I'll bring the noodles and the wine. Please call me at beeper 89647."

"Yes, please," she whispered when he called her back. "I'd like that very much."

THEY WERE LOCKED in a frantic embrace an instant after she opened the door. Lucretia felt great joy and vast relief. This was right, absolutely right for her—and for him, too.

"Now look here!" he said when they'd finished the noodles from the ground-floor eating shop and were sipping the second bottle of Beaujolais from Oliver's. "I'm sorry, very sorry. I've been playing ducks and drakes with you. You heard me right the other day. I *am* going to Tibet. I've *got* to! Damned nuisance, but I've got no choice. Can you forgive me for stalling . . . for not telling you outright earlier?"

She already believed Robbie was all-important in her life. She now knew he was even more than that. He was essential to her being, as essential as her right arm. You could, of course, lose your right arm and survive. She could, perhaps, survive without Robbie, just barely. But what kind of life would that be? Undoubtedly barren, bleak, and icy—endlessly depressing, one long dark night of the spirit. Overcome by her own fantasy, Lucretia felt chilled, and she shuddered. At once plaintive and indignant, she demanded, "Why did you wait so long to tell me? Why *must* you go?"

"I couldn't say any more then. It wasn't my secret. I had to get permission, and that took awhile. . . . Why go? Because it's vital, to me and to many others. Besides, I've given my word."

"As long as I know you're coming back to me, I'll manage," she said slowly. "But how I'll live for weeks without you, not knowing where you are or how you are . . ."

"Of course I'll come back, just as fast as I can. I'll try to keep in touch, but there're no postboxes on the high plateau of Tibet. All letters go straight to the Chinese Public Security Bureau."

"That's not funny!" Yet she smiled as she protested. "So many weeks without you."

"Maybe more. We've got to face up to it. Travel in Tibet's very slow. I'll be away at least a month, maybe two."

Lucretia's heart sank, but she put her arms around his neck and urged, "It's *your* choice. If you don't *want* to go, don't go. You only have to say *No!*"

"I can't say *No,* no matter how much I'd like to. That would be treachery, betraying my people, my religion, and His Holiness, the Dalai Lama. That I *cannot* do!"

"And this vital mission?" Lucretia demanded. "It's more important to you than . . . than *me?*"

"Of course it's not more important. Just a little errand for my country . . . for Tibet. Safe as houses, no derring-do."

"Why you? Why does it have to be you?"

Robbie responded softly, " 'I could not love thee, dear, so much, loved I not honor more!' The poet got it about right."

"Do tell me what it's all about," Lucretia said. "Also, why do you talk one way in public about the Chinese and another way when it's just the two of us?"

"Why do you think I've been so careful not to offend Beijing or the Communists' running dogs in Hong Kong? I even let that jackal H. K. Lam have his undersize girders. Full certification, though it stuck in my craw. What else could I do?"

He bowed his head and knuckled his eyes. Studying her face intently, he said, "You've twigged, haven't you? I've been pandering to Beijing and its running dogs. To learn what's really going to happen to Hong Kong. And so I could travel freely in China. . . . But I wouldn't let them frighten me away from you."

"I'm so glad," she replied.

"But what's the payoff?"

"It's for Tibet . . . for the future of my country. And, of course, for the Dalai Lama. He's not only the pope of Tantric Buddhism, but much more. He's the fourteenth reincarnation as Dalai Lama of Chenrezig, the Compassionate, the Profoundly Compassionate Buddha who is, as you'd say, the patron saint of Tibet.

"His Holiness is a demigod. A god king, the West calls him, oversimplifying as usual. He's also our sovereign, our king or our president for life. He's responsible for the earthly as well as the spiritual well-being of all Tibetans wherever they may be."

"Why is the Dalai Lama fixated on South China?"

"Because China's vital to our future. Because China is occupying Tibet, killing our patriots, destroying our religion, savaging our civilization."

"Why South China in particular?"

"South China could be the model of China's future. Industry is growing there like toadstools after the rain. His Holiness must know: What is the mood of the people, the strengths and the weakness of local governments, the temper of the officials? Are the provinces, the regions, breaking away from Beijing? Only when he has all the facts can he shape his policies—and lead Tibet to independence again."

"You send reports all the time, don't you? Why do you have to go to him?"

"I'm only a cog, but His Holiness wants to get my impressions direct. The nuances are hard to get down on paper. And I do as I'm told."

"Why Lhasa afterward?" Lucretia persisted. "Why not come back and pick up your daily work and your reporting?"

"There's also meetings to keep the resistance alive. I'm meant to brief guerrilla leaders in Gyantse and Lhasa."

"All right, darling, I surrender. I see I can't move you, can't begin to change your mind, so I'll stop heckling. All I can say is God bless you . . . and bring you home safe very soon."

Resigned, if not wholly content, Lucretia opened her arms to him. For some time, there was no use for them to say a word; talk would have been intrusive. Afterward when they sat on the balcony overlooking the glowing nighttime panorama of Victoria and Kowloon, she was confident he would return as swiftly as he could. No man could fake the exaltation to which their lovemaking raised Robbie.

"I've got to leave right now. I should've left yesterday, a week ago," he said. "After October it's tricky traveling by bus through the Himalayas."

"By bus? Why not fly? Much quicker."

"I'm flying to New Delhi on a charter airline that's dirt cheap. You know, I'll probably have to foot the bill myself. Even the Dalai can't spend money he hasn't got."

"Can't you fly from India?"

"The Chinese Public Security Police go over everyone who gets off a plane in Lhasa with a fine-tooth comb. A Tibetan carrying a full British passport is an oddity, certain to attract attention. I don't want them to know about my arrival. This way, I'll be just another dumb Tibetan pilgrim on foot who stops off to make obeisance to the Dalai Lama."

Lucretia was not happy with his answers. Everyone, even Robbie himself, seemed to be conspiring to keep them apart. He was not all that anxious to cut his trip short.

Throwing aside dull routine for this adventure obviously stirred him. And why not? He was as eager as a cub scout before his first overnight hike. The lure was not hot dogs burnt over a fire, but *tsampa,* coarse ground barley, and salted tea laced with yak butter that was the staple of travelers in Tibet. Also *chang,* the heavy, powerful beer made from barley. Why in Heaven's name should he want to end his adventure before it even began?

Lucretia shifted on the white cushions of the cane settee. Tucking her legs under herself, she moved closer, and Robbie put his arm around her. She was wearing only a thin cotton robe, and he only a towel tied around his waist. But she was not out to arouse him. Their lovemaking was over until his return.

Not that her body would not ache for his hands. Not that she would not feel empty without him. Yet, above all, she would miss him as the rock upon which her renewed self-confidence rested.

Lucretia moved closer and put her head on his shoulder to assure him of her love and her loyalty. When his arm tightened around her, she realized that her gesture was meant just as much to reassure herself that he loved her and would without fail return.

Still, she wondered uneasily about Robbie's grandmother, who retained her authority, though he had not seen her for thirty years. Why had she summoned Robbie? Only because she wanted to see him again before she died? Or was there more to it?

"Robbie," she asked casually, "why does your grandmother want to see you?"

"Family solidarity, I imagine . . . Continuity, that sort of thing. She's not getting any younger, eighty if she's a day. It's only natural."

"Such a long way just to give her a glimpse of you?"

"Wouldn't your grandmother want to see you? You know, Lucretia, sometimes I think you deliberately fail to understand family ties in Asia. That's reason enough, quite enough, even if—"

"Even if *what*, Robbie? Sounds as if there's more to it than just sentiment."

She had to know if there *were* anything else behind his going to Lhasa. Otherwise, she would brood and fret and imagine dire scenarios during all the time he was away. She glanced up and saw that he was rubbing his eyes with his knuckles.

"There is something else, isn't there, Robbie? I know there is!"

"It's tied up with filial piety, with the family," he at last replied. "To be honest, she's after me to marry. Her letters keep reminding me I'm not getting any younger. Thirty-nine, she says, is high time to marry and have children. Past time! I reckon she wants to tell me the same thing in person—to pressure me!"

"What a good idea!" Lucretia laughed. "Just what I'd recommend! High time you married and had children. When do we do the deed?"

"You don't understand, Lucretia!" He responded neither to her jokey tone nor to her underlying earnestness. "How could you possibly understand?"

"People get married every day. And here I am, ready and willing."

"You're only making it worse, Lucretia. She's already picked out the bride. Of course, it's *not* you. Grandmother's never heard of you. How could she?"

He paused momentarily and resumed grimly, "You might as well hear the rest. The Tibetan community here has also picked out a bride for me. Not the same as Grandmother's choice, of course."

"How galling for you, Robbie. She still wasn't taking him seriously. "Naturally, you've told them not to be foolish."

"It's not that simple, dear. They demand I marry a *Tibetan*. Anyone else is unthinkable. If I marry a non-Tibetan, they say I'll be cut off from the Tibetan community, from our religion as well. Doesn't matter whether she's Chinese, English, or American, they say. Regardless, I'll become an outcast, an apostate."

"You, an apostate? That's ridiculous! Do they think I'm going to convert you? To what? Agnosticism? More likely you'll convert me."

"They're not all wrong, Lucretia. In a way, it is a choice between Tibet and the outside world."

Lucretia was thunderstruck—and appalled. Tearful, she asked,

"You mean you're thinking of . . . you'll just let them tell you what to do? I can't believe I'm hearing you right, Robbie."

"Of course not! Not if I can help it. But sometimes things are inevitable, written in the book of fate. Besides, no matter what happens, it won't affect us. We'll still be the same to each other. I'll always love only you. I swear it."

Lucretia freed herself from Robbie's arm and turned to face him. She was now kneeling on the settee, her eyes level with his. She gazed into his shadowed green eyes and wondered if she'd ever truly understood this man. Was he really as naive, as ingenuous, as he appeared at this moment? Or, not to mince words, was he faking? Was he only pretending not to comprehend her anxiety? This deliberate deceit, as it must be, this was monstrous.

"I can't believe it, Robbie!" She spoke very slowly, tautly self-controlled, though she felt on the verge of hysteria. "Please tell me you're joking! Of course, that is it! You're only testing me—in a very cruel way."

"I'm afraid not." Harried, ashamed, and perplexed, he shook his head. "That's what they want."

"And you? What do *you* want, Robbie, *really* want?"

"I want you, Lucretia, my only darling, only you. I want you for all my life."

"So then?" She was almost brusque in her dawning relief from the horror she had felt a moment earlier. "Why not . . ."

"I always want to be part of the Tibetan community. I can't turn my back on them."

"All right, then," she agreed. "We'll just stay right here. I'll bury my revulsion at the worst sides of Hong Kong. After all, only a few things really get to me. We'll stay right here—and you'll be just as you've always been."

"No, Lucretia!" His voice cracked, and his words came with agonizing slowness. "It won't work that way. What would our children be? Hardly Tibetan! The mother shapes the children. And ours would be Western, very Western: American or British—not just by blood, but by upbringing. No, it won't work. There's a lot in what they say, Grandmother and the Hong Kong Old Lama."

"Well, then?" Despite herself, Lucretia's tone was astringent, even harsh, for her heart was hammering furiously. She was terrified, on the edge of panic. Looking down the long gray corridors of the future, she saw herself: a pale solitary figure, always alone, bereft of the only man she had ever truly loved. Sure, she was a modern woman, feisty and independent—but she was so damned dependent on Robbie.

"It needn't be that way," he said haltingly. "There's an alternative! We could still be together."

"How, Robbie?"

Hope welled again in her heart. Was he, after all, prepared to defy the racist taboos of the medieval code of behavior hammered into him by barbaric lamas in ultramodern Hong Kong?

"Now, there're some curious Tibetan customs you've probably read about," he continued. "Like one woman's marrying all the brothers in a family to ensure the property isn't split up. Not only polyandry, one wife and several husbands. Also polygamy, one husband and several wives when necessary. Such are our customs. So, basically, it doesn't matter who I marry, which Tibetan girl, either or both. You'll always be first in my heart and in my arms . . . another true wife."

Her hopes shattered on his granite insensitivity, Lucretia replied after a moment, "Even Hong Kong abolished polygamy a couple of decades ago. Do you know what you're really asking? You're asking me to be your mistress, a self-supporting mistress. You could barely support a wife, much less a mistress. But you'll have your cozy little Tibetan household while I . . . I live in some hovel, waiting for my lord and master to spare a moment to come and see me."

"It's not like that at all!"

"Then what *is* it like?" Her voice was brittle. "What would we do, then? How would we live?"

"I haven't thought it through, but surely—"

"I feel unclean, used and exploited. You've methodically deceived me. You've violated me. Lord knows, I was ready to do without marriage. It's only a formality, marriage. But this . . . this is monstrous. You're to marry someone else—and I'm to be your chief mistress. How you could ever . . ."

"I don't expect you to understand immediately," he said. "I know how shocked and angry you are. And I'm ashamed. I'm so desperately sorry. I do love you, God knows. I'll love you, only you, forever. It tears at my heart to see you so disturbed, so despairing, in such a fury."

"The solution's very simple, Robbie!"

"You still don't understand. I'm stuck with it, caught like a rabbit in a trap. I'm being torn apart by opposing loyalties. I can't turn my back on Tibet. I can't just tip my hat and say to His Holiness, It's been fun, but I'm pulling out now! That would make a mockery of everything I've lived for. My life would be meaningless. *I* would be meaningless. How could we be happy then?"

"But you're happy to propose I become your mistress, no more. Happy to make my life meaningless while you raise a proper cozy little Tibetan family with a Tibetan wife or two. I'm supposed to sacrifice everything while you sacrifice nothing at all. What's become of the gallant, charming, modern-minded, independent lover I thought I knew so well?"

They were glaring at each other like avowed enemies, rather than sworn lovers. He looked away, but she still stared at him, her light-blue eyes indigo with accusation.

"God knows I can do without formal marriage," she said softly. "Almost happily do without marriage. But for you to take a wife while I . . . That's insulting and demeaning. It's monstrous!"

'I'll tell you what," he at last offered. "I promise I won't . . . won't make any commitment. No commitment of any kind until I come back and we can talk it all over."

"I suppose that's better than nothing," she responded reluctantly. "I suppose I should be grateful . . . and I suppose I am." He smiled in relief, but she went on, "You do know what you're leaving me with, don't you? Weeks, maybe months of agonizing. I can't swear in return. I won't promise I'll wait for you like a Victorian heroine. I just don't know, Robbie!"

II

DORJE RABNET, KNOWN in his world as Robbie, vanished with the dawn of the next day to reappear elsewhere under another name. He telephoned from Kai Tak Airport minutes before his flight boarded to bid Lucretia a loving good-bye. He found her cool and unresponsive. Yet he assured her once again that he would come back to her just as soon as he could—subject, of course, to the instructions of the Dalai Lama and the wishes of his grandmother.

Robbie's words, like his tone, assumed that everything between Lucretia and himself was unaltered. Yet they had little to say to each other, nothing practical to discuss and, on her part, no endearments to offer. Lucretia did not restate in so many words her distrust of his promises, but her brusqueness carried its own message.

How could she possibly trust his renewed promises after he

had been so devious and so dilatory in telling her of his journey? Had she not had to winkle out of him the news that he was under pressure to marry a Tibetan girl? How could she possibly consider his proposition that she become his second or even third wife under the sanction of Tibetan polygamy? Not his first wife, however, for that lady's chief duty would be to produce Tibetan children.

His proposition was not only odious; it was impossible. Hong Kong law forbade polygamy in any guise. He was baldly proposing that she continue to sleep with him while he conducted his family life elsewhere.

In Lucretia's eyes Robbie's departure was final. He had lied to her once too often, even if his were entirely lies of omission. Those lies had cracked the bedrock of mutual candor on which their love had rested.

Lying awake through the gray hours of many mornings, she strove to reassure herself with flimsy illusions. In the daylight hours, she could find no reason to believe he would return to fan the embers of a dying love. Even if he did, her torch would never flame again. It was cold and dead.

Robbie and she were through. Theirs had proved to be no more than a brief affair—and the affair was over.

Such was Lucretia's melancholy conviction when Robbie vanished in the direction of New Delhi on an ancient Boeing 707 chartered by Friendship Air Tours. Thirty-seven years in service, the airplane had lately flown for offbeat airlines like Air Patagonia and Royal Air Cambodge. Its reliability was questionable, a disgruntled stewardess told him, for the hand-to-mouth charter company was skimping on both maintenance and pilot costs.

Robbie's fears might more realistically have focused on Lucretia, to whom he owed not only his new poise and his new self-confidence, but his new happiness. Yet he hardly thought of her after the 707 took off. He had the seasoned traveler's knack of sweeping from his mind all concern regarding his homebase as soon as he boarded an airplane. Besides, he was totally caught up by the adventure on which he was setting forth.

Robbie vanished like an Olympic diver whose swift entry into the water leaves hardly a ripple on the surface. Eagerly looking forward to his audience with the Dalai Lama and his first sight of Lhasa in three decades, he was hardly aware that he had left a jagged rift in Lucretia's life.

BEFORE HER DISASTROUS marriage, Lucretia Hatton had supported herself by selling her paintings and giving private lessons, whether in Cambridge, New York, or, for a time, in London. In Hong Kong, her income from the occasional sale of a painting and her part-time teaching at the Chinese University could not pay the rent on a decent one-bedroom apartment.

Why should she be valued by relentlessly commercial Hong Kong? She was neither an heiress nor a predator; neither a purveyor of useless luxuries to the super-rich nor a designer of bizarre and ludicrously expensive clothes; neither a rapacious interior decorator nor a money magician, not even an exorbitantly priced courtesan.

Shortly before she met Robbie she had, rather foolishly it now appeared, turned down an offer to be a billionaire's official mistress. She had sternly rejected both the luxury and the security. How moral! How principled! How fastidious and righteous! How stupid!

Now that Robbie had deserted her, she wondered briefly whether she could get that proposition renewed. The billionaire had offered a fully staffed five-bedroom apartment on the Peak, as well a a chauffeured Rolls-Royce convertible, a hundred-ten-foot yacht, and other fringe benefits.

She badly needed a windfall now. She would not even have a place to live when the owners returned to claim back the apartment she was caretaking.

LUCRETIA DID NOT, however, revel in despair. Neither necessity nor her own temperament allowed her to brood on the collapse of her hopes for happiness with Dorje Rabnet. She still had her own life to manage as best she could.

Lucretia felt sorry for Robbie, hog-tied as he was by filial piety and Buddhist piety. He would return to face the bleak task of finding another sanctuary for Althea Garland Rabnet, since the Hong Kong Sanatorium was to be razed. Though it was an old-fashioned notion, she believed that care of the aged was far better handled with feminine sensitivity than with masculine ham-fistedness. But she sternly told herself to stop worrying about Robbie and worry about herself.

Calling herself again Lucretia Hatton, she found that she'd by no means entirely lost the self-confidence Robbie had cultivated. Somehow, dropping the name Barnes was a victory in itself. If not wholly a new woman, she was at least a refurbished model of the original woman, for she had regained her independence of spirit.

She energetically set out to see more of her friends. Except for an occasional party, she had all but abandoned those friends for Robbie. She also threw herself into her work for the Democratic Party. Opposed to Beijing's tyranny, the Democrats were savagely denounced by Beijing. Her posters caricaturing Beijing's spokesmen on Hong Kong and their local lackeys were applauded by the mass of the people—and she enjoyed her small fame.

Lucretia of course knew that her forceful attacks on tomorrow's rulers were making it ever less likely that she would be allowed to stay in Hong Kong after June 30, 1997. But that no longer mattered.

Her posters, which she signed *Hatton* beside a stick drawing of a woman wearing a big hat, were also her declaration of independence from Robbie. How could an ostensible "friend" of the Beijing regime be the lover, much less the husband, of an acid critic of that regime?

Yet, who could say exactly how Hong Kong's new rulers would behave? There was apparently no precedent. Nothing remotely similar had ever occurred. Never had a democratic country like Britain voluntarily delivered seven million subjects to a tyrannical dictatorship! Never had the rich, the entrepreneurs, the managers, the professional classes, and the natural leaders of the community thus betrayed and abandoned the common people.

The wisest men and women in Hong Kong itself had over the decades signally failed to anticipate what China would do next. Only fools now argued that Beijing must honor its pledge to give the former Colony fifty years of semi-autonomy with unchanged economic and social systems—because of the pressure of world opinion and also because Beijing would not kill the goose that laid the golden eggs. Just so had Old Hong Kong hands assured each other decades earlier that the Communists would never demand direct control of the Colony, but would preserve it as a separate entity under British rule because it was so useful to them.

In truth, no one really *knew* what Beijing would do once Hong Kong belonged to China. The future was up for grabs.

Lucretia's belief that the change would be disastrous was based only on intuition. There was no objective evidence to support the red fat cats' loud assertion that Beijing's rule would make the territory even more prosperous.

Yet Lucretia found right next door someone who could relate Hong Kong's future to the past. She always enjoyed her chats with old Selma Lotz, who lived just across the elevator landing. But she hardly expected the seventy-seven-year-old widow to offer a unique insight into the future of Hong Kong in the light of Shanghai's past.

Selma Lotz had become her confidante, for the old lady was as wise and dispassionate as a great-aunt to whom she could tell everything, even things she couldn't tell her mother. Selma had smiled sadly when Lucretia told her the full story of Robbie's perfidy. Yet her advice had been a surprise.

"Lucretia, my dear," she'd said, "whatever your Robbie's done, whatever grudge you hold, you obviously love him very much. If he comes back to you, don't ever let him go again. Just hang on to him!"

Robbie had not returned. He had vanished just five weeks before that rainy late November afternoon, and there had since then been not a word from him—or of him.

Lucretia broke off work on a poster that showed Lu Ping, director of Beijing's Office for Hong Kong and Macau, holding a garden hose from which gushed a crystal substance labeled *Freedom*. Those who rushed with buckets to collect a little freedom were turned back by heavily armed Liberation Army soldiers, and the crystal stream ran into a swamp labeled *Beijing Dictatorship*.

Crude, Lucretia concluded, but effective—even more effective when the simple captions were put into Chinese characters. She was now ready for the iced tea and the chocolate chip cookies promised by Mrs. Lotz, who'd learned to make them from her American daughter-in-law.

Ensconced in the cane peacock-tail chair she loved, Lucretia stretched wearily and confided, "Instinct tells me—common sense tells me—the Communists'll be bad, very bad, for Hong Kong. But it's only a gut feeling. I don't really *know*. Far as I can see, no one knows."

Selma Lotz popped a sprig of mint into the pitcher of iced tea. Her hands then went to the pure white hair that framed her remarkably unlined face. She was vain about her luxuriant hair and her youthful features, little touched by the strains of a turbulent life. After those diversions, she spoke in an accent that owed more to her schooling by English and French nuns in Shanghai than to her Russian Jewish origins.

"Lucretia, dear, *I'll* tell you!" Selma Lotz said. "It's no great mystery. . . .

"I always thought I'd die in China or, at least, in Hong Kong. Not that I'm in a hurry to die. But, when death came, I wanted to meet him here. You know, China's been my life.

"No longer! Another two months—and we're leaving, all of us: my two boys with their wives and, naturally, all seven kids. My girl Doris, too, though her husband wanted to stay. I just couldn't stand to see again in Hong Kong what I already saw once in Shanghai."

Lucretia already knew something of Selma Lotz's past. The old lady's parents had fled Russia in the late 1920s when "bourgeois elements" were purged. Settling in Harbin in Manchuria, far to the north, her father had gone into the fur trade—and made a very good living. Selma had been ten years old when the family came to Harbin. After a few years, Japanese-engineered unrest had driven them out of Manchuria, along with thousands of other Russian refugees, including a gaggle of emphatically non-Jewish princes, countesses, and generals. The International Settlement in Shanghai was the only place in Asia, perhaps the entire world, that did not reject refugees who possessed neither passports nor visas.

"I think," Selma Lotz recalled, "they wanted to balance the Chinese population with more Europeans. Whatever the reason, they welcomed the Russian refugees, even the Jews. A little later, they also welcomed hundreds, maybe thousands, of refugees from Hitler's Germany, almost all Jewish. The Settlement had to set up a Jewish company of the Shanghai Volunteers, our little toy army, alongside American, Dutch, and British companies.

"The biggest changes were in medicine and music. Every other German Jew, it seemed, was a doctor. Lawyers and bankers didn't get out so easily. So, many more sick people were treated in Shanghai.

"Also, it seemed every other doctor carried a violin saved from the Nazi gangsters. Those without fiddles had trumpets or cornets or French horns. And three dignified Herr Doktors lugged enormous bass violins. Naturally, the pianists, a half dozen or so, came empty-handed. There were plenty of pianos in the Settlement. Soon cinema orchestras were mostly Jewish, mostly doctors. And Shanghai had a really good symphony orchestra for the first time."

Lucretia smiled. She'd already heard parts of the tale. She knew that in 1937, at the age of eighteen, Selma had married a Russian

Jewish refugee who changed his name from Mendel Lotzowkof-sky as a wedding present to his bride. The newly minted Max Lotz was a jeweler. Taking advantage of minuscule Chinese wages and great Chinese skills, he manufactured and exported reasonably priced costume jewelry to Europe and America.

"We lived through the Japanese attacks and the Japanese occupation," Selma Lotz resumed. "It was terrible, heart-breaking. All the slaughter, the bombing and the shelling, and half Shanghai in flames, naturally the Chinese part. The International Settlement was reasonably safe till the Japs marched in on December eighth, 1941.

"Max and I could go about our business practically untouched. Only when Hitler insisted did the Japs intern stateless Jews like us. But their hearts weren't in it. They weren't rough. Why should they get so involved in some crazy quarrel among Europeans?

"The war ended—and we stayed on. The factory reopened, and life was very pleasant again. But the Kuomintang, the Nationalists, were fighting a losing battle against the Communists. Being Jewish liberals and idealists, we were naturally for the Communists. When the People's Liberation Army marched into Shanghai in 1949, we stood on the sidewalks and cheered."

Selma Lotz smiled to herself, as if reliving those halcyon days. She smiled and patted her white hair into place and shifted her slender frame in her own peacock chair.

"Lucretia, my dear, you can't imagine how exciting it was," she said. "Everything looked wonderful. Mao Zedong said he wasn't bringing Communism, not even Socialism, but only the New Democracy. He talked about coalition government and convened the People's Political Consultative Conference to get advice and support from non-Communists. And he promised that all capitalists could keep doing business, just as long as they weren't what he called 'bureaucratic capitalists,' who'd sided with the Nationalists and made millions from dirty dealing. A new day was dawning, and the sky was bright over old Shanghai."

Her lips curled in a rueful smile, she went on, "Of course, it was all a fraud. Mao didn't mean a word he said. He was a very good liar. You know, the Communists believe lying for their cause is their sacred duty.

"Max and I, we kept the factory going till 1952. Other foreigners were being deported—after paying ransoms to 'compensate' employees for having exploited them. And more millions to 'make restitution for stealing from the Chinese people.' But we weren't touched. Max had always paid fair wages. God knows, they were low enough.

"Only business wasn't very good. The Communists were cutting China off from the world. So bang went our main markets abroad. And no Chinese was buying jewelry, not even costume jewelry. The Communists demanded proletarian simplicity, plain clothing with no ornaments, certainly no jewelry. Most were hicks and yokels, primitive puritans from the farms who believed austerity and sacrifice and living uncomfortably were great virtues in themselves. For the people, of course, not for the Communist bosses.

"In 1952, three years after the Liberation Army marched in, the bubble burst. The Communists were purging their own ranks—cadres who'd been corrupted by wicked businessmen in the wicked cities. They called it Three Anti's, this purge, for the three big sins the capitalists tempted the cadres to commit: theft, bribery, and selling state secrets.

"Next came the Five Anti's to punish the five big sins that

businessmen and capitalists were committing. Protest was whipped up by Communist cadres, who came into the factory from outside.

"Max they locked up in his own office, giving him only a bite of food from time to time, just enough to keep him going. They were after him night and day to confess to his crimes. They heckled and jeered at him as a foreign imperialist capitalist exploiter. They beat drums and crashed cymbals in his ears day and night. They pounded on pots and pans, never stopping. They gave him only a cup of water and maybe a spoonful of cold rice a day— and they never stopped shouting at him. They didn't treat him gently, but they didn't beat him up the way they did Chinese businessmen. Only a couple of slaps and, maybe, a punch or two. Many Chinese they drove to suicide.

"Most of our old workers smiled in shame or shrugged in apology when the Communist cadres weren't watching. They wanted to show they were acting against their will. If they hadn't persecuted Max and made up lies about him, they would've been attacked themselves.

"After two weeks, Max cracked. He told me later he would've confessed to rape or murder if they'd asked him, he was so tired and confused. So he confessed to stealing state secrets, corrupting Communist cadres with bribes, and embezzling the people's wealth.

"Then the Communists were 'lenient.' Or so they said. They confiscated everything except the clothes we stood up in and shipped the whole family out to Hong Kong. Easiest move we ever made. No belongings, no furniture or clothes, nothing to worry about except ourselves."

"You stayed in Hong Kong, and you prospered," Lucretia said. "Why run away now?"

"Because it's going to be the same. Maybe it'll take longer for the crackdown than the three years it took in Shanghai, maybe not so long. But sometime in the next five or six years the Communists'll crack down. Not exactly the same persecution as the Five Anti's. No campaign to destroy private enterprise because the Communists themselves are the biggest exploiting capitalists nowadays. Maybe no campaign against corruption because the Communists are even more corrupt now, all rotten to the core. But everything else the same.

"They're promising no change in the capitalist system for fifty years the way they promised Shanghai capitalists could keep doing business. No Communism for Hong Kong, they say, but the same system as always, just like they promised the New Democracy for Shanghai. And a powerless rubber-stamp Preparatory Commission to bring in all the fellow travelers and opportunists—and make the transition look halfway democratic, just like the People's Political Consultative Congress in 1949.

"First they'll get your precious Democratic Party. The Communists see it as a lot of licensed counterrevolutionaries. Of course, the press'll be free, the Communists say, free to report facts, though not to advocate nonofficial views or to comment adversely. Naturally not free to undermine the government with criticism or to question China's sovereignty over Hong Kong. In other words, total freedom to follow the Communist line.

"Also schoolbooks will be cleansed of the 'errors and lies' inserted by the imperialist exploiters. Teachers will learn to follow the 'correct' line. There won't be any 'bourgeois' freedom of speech, expression, or even thought. But the Communists say everything else will remain the same.

"Except they'll abolish the Legislative Council, replace it with their puppet Provisional Legislature. It's too free, too outspoken, too anti-Beijing, the legislature we elected last year. The Communists have the nerve to say the British've given Hong Kong too much democracy. *No* democracy at all is what they like.

"And, even the highest court will be 'given political guidance,' just like the courts in China. That means no legal system can work. In the long run no protection by law and no free businesses can operate. Yet the Communists say everything will be the same!

"So many promises, just like Shanghai. But they're already doing almost exactly the same as they did in Shanghai.

"Sometimes I think it's a blessing Max is dead, not to have to suffer again. Once is enough for a lifetime! Do you wonder we're leaving?"

12

THERE WAS SO much about the Colony Lucretia had grown to love: the opportunities it offered its youth; the acceptance of responsibility that had put up half the population in government housing because private housing was not available for the poor; the concern for culture that had provided universities and polytechnics in some numbers, as well as stage and music academies, all virtually free; the science and art museums; the supple adaptability that had enabled the Colony to survive triumphantly the tumultuous and dangerous years since 1949. Above all, she loved the cocky, irrepressible spirit of its people.

The Colony was a unique self-contained community that had sprung from its own roots, neither China's nor Britain's. It had not only saved millions from oppression and degradation, but had also engaged the higher aspirations. It was *sui generis,* a unique creation virtually a self-creation, neither British nor Chinese, but itself.

Why else than for love of the Colony should she linger, reluctant to leave? It could not be solely to wait for Robbie. She had thrust him out of her heart, she assured herself, despite the longing that assailed her. Anyway, there was no possibility of reviving their moribund affair, even if she had wanted to. Besides, so much time had gone by that hope of his reappearing was dwindling.

A cheerless Christmas had already passed and a New Year's Eve that held out little hope for the future, either Lucretia's own or the Colony's. She had rarely been alone during the festive season, but had usually been surrounded by a crush of merrymakers. New Year's Eve had been diversely celebrated: sodden and quarrelsome at the Foreign Correspondents Club; flamboyant and expensive at the Peninsula Hotel; boisterous and dangerous in the younger foreigners' enclave of Lan Kwai Fong. But Lucretia had felt alone among the rambunctious throngs.

In bleak late January of the fatal year 1997, the last Lunar New Year's festivities under the British flag were approaching. Four hundred electors handpicked by the Communists had chosen a multimillionaire ship owner born in Shanghai, who was deep in Beijing's debt, to be Hong Kong's next Chief Executive—and the Communists had hailed that rubber-stamping as a triumph of democracy, the first time the people of Hong Kong had had a voice in choosing their governor. Such portents pointed to a tense New Year celebration, a bittersweet farewell to more than a century and a half of British rule and a reluctant, fearful welcome to the new Chinese overlords. All Hong Kong would let itself go—perhaps for the last time.

As though Lucretia was an outsider who told herself she intended to leave Hong Kong before the fatal day, she, too, was unsettled and edgy. Above all, she wanted to see Robbie again, even if he were unlikely to reappear. Even if he were to reappear with an apple-cheeked Tibetan chit on his arm, she would, at least, no longer have to worry about his fate. But was that really true?

Despite her devoted labors for the Democratic Party and the Alliance for Democracy in China, drawing posters and cartoons, writing speeches for those whose English was weak, even stuffing envelopes; despite her teaching at the Chinese University; despite her frenzied bouts of painting; despite her busy social life—she still missed him.

"Dammit!" she confessed aloud in her bedroom. "I do miss the conniving son of a bitch, no matter how he's behaved."

Lucretia heard her own words and abruptly realized that she was no longer brooding resentfully on Robbie's cavalier behavior. She also realized that she was no longer infuriated or absolutely determined to expel him from her life. If she were still angry, why would she be agonizing over his fate?

Then, she recalled, there was Jacobus. She smiled deprecatingly at this new notion. An instant later she saw that it was neither foolish nor trivial. She could have borne Robbie's ominously protracted absence more easily if he'd left Jacobus for her to look after. Sentimental it might sound to some, even ridiculous. But the golden shih-tzu with the black face would have been a great comfort—and an implicit promise that his master would return. Had they not briefly been a family, Robbie, Jacobus, and herself?

But Jacobus, too, had disappeared. None of Robbie's neighbors could tell her what had become of the lion dog.

THAT MID-JANUARY day, while Lucretia in Hong Kong regarded the future bleakly, a small bus painted electric green was creeping south from Lhasa along the dark thread of the road that stitched together horizonless wastes studded with dingy outcrops of sand, withered straw-colored vegetation, and dirty-gray rocks. In the dull light of late afternoon, the bus shone iridescent like an opal: gold and silver, red, orange, and blue against a brilliant green background.

Even in deep winter a few heavily laden buses each week made the seven-hundred-mile journey from Lhasa, the capital of Tibet, to Kathmandu, the capital of Nepal. They rolled with relative ease across the arid High Plateau, which was normally devoid of snow, since the temperature varied from well below freezing, say six degrees Fahrenheit at night, to ninety Fahrenheit at high noon. When sandstorms or blizzards struck, buses sheltered behind the nearest heights, natural or manmade. Farther south, however, they struggled to get through passes as high as eighteen thousand feet, just above the permanent snow line and well above the tree line.

Some buses were defeated by deep-piled snow in the passes. But they usually got through. If a bus bogged down in a pass that was only partially cleared, twenty or so able-bodied men would jump out to level the snowbanks and push the stranded vehicle until it regained traction. Since every man was accompanied by at least one wife and many by two or three children as well, their belongings normally overflowed the baggage compartment. The excess was roped to the roof. But this bus was unencumbered, as well as highly polished.

On the front bench sat a tall man wearing a chocolate-colored fedora made in Tianjin on the China coast. The fedora was pulled down, shading his eyes. A sprinkling of Tibetans had green eyes like Dorje Rabnet's, relics of Mongol or Turkic invaders over the centuries. It was, nonetheless, prudent to conceal his eyes and thus avoid arousing curiosity. Two men seated behind him wore similar Tianjin fedoras similarly pulled down to shadow their faces. All three wore the felt *chuba,* a heavy cloak belted at the waist, which normally left one shoulder bare. All three had drawn their cloaks over their shoulders against the biting cold creeping into the bus as twilight approached.

A slight monk in a saffron chuba said his prayers with eyes downcast, the eighteen carved faces that were the beads of his rosary clicking as he completed each cycle. Behind him two women adorned with cascades of necklaces gossiped in loud voices, ignoring the men. Their faces, permanently chapped by the harsh climate, glowed even brighter red as the cold twined itself around them.

The heating system was fitful, even in this special bus provided by the underground resistance of Gyantse for their important visitor. That gesture embarrassed Robbie and worried him. He feared the virtually private bus would make him conspicuous— and invite closer inspection by the Chinese Public Security Police and the Chinese army of occupation. But the resistance leaders had assured him that this bus regularly plied the Nepal route. Aside from the two bodyguards, who were to see him safe to Kathmandu, the only unusual touch was the excessive cleanliness. He had been further assured that Tibetan bus drivers were learning that relatively clean buses were good for business.

Robbie was returning to Kathmandu in the character of a prosperous merchant, the relative comfort of this journey homeward quite different from his earlier trek into Tibet. Leaving his British passport with the Dalai Lama in Dharamsala in northern India, he had carried a *laissez passer* that identified him as a poor and pious pilgrim to the Buddhist shrines of his homeland.

Because the pilgrim could not afford bus fare, Robbie had walked and hitchhiked. He had even been forced to accept a lift from a Liberation Army truck, lest he arouse suspicion by turning down the driver's unusual kindness to a native. He had traveled very slowly, resting for a day or two between stages. Regardless of his Tibetan blood, Robbie, like any new arrival, particularly a new arrival from muggy sea-level Hong Kong, needed time to adjust to the increasing altitude and the constantly diminishing oxygen in the progressively thinner air. The alternative to delay could be altitude sickness, which was sometimes fatal.

He had been happy to follow a leisurely, circuitous route. Sustaining his role as a pilgrim, he had visited the major shrines along the road to burn incense sticks and light votive lamps whose wicks floated in liquid butter. He was in truth a reverent pilgrim.

When he paused at a deserted shrine near Gyantse, the wind was wailing through rifts in the walls and through splintered doorways. The abbess of that convent, Tibet's only female reincarnation, had been known as Dorje Phagmo, the Thunderbolt Sow, a title at which even the reverent Robbie smiled.

Centuries earlier, Mongol besiegers had broken into the convent to find no humans, but many pigs. When they sheathed their swords, they were awed by seeing the pigs transformed into the holy abbess among her nuns and monks. Sadly, the last reincarnation had renounced her semidivinity to live as an ordinary mortal.

One of the saddest sights on his inward trek was Tibet's second largest city, Shigatse, with its forty thousand people and its massive Tashilhunpo Monastery. Following the clockwise pilgrims' circuit around the monastery walls, Robbie looked down on a city that had all but lost its Tibetan character since the Chinese occupation in 1950. Shigatse was now a depressing gray town of solid, square, grimy, utilitarian, modern Chinese buildings.

The Tashilhunpo Monastery was also depressing. Its four thousand monks had dwindled to five hundred, who still prayed before the great image of Maitreya, the Buddha of the Future, seventy feet high and sheathed with six hundred pounds of gold. The Monastery had been founded by the first Dalai Lama five centuries earlier, but its showpiece was the gold-roofed tomb of the fourth incarnation of the Panchen Lama. Nearby stood the vacant Throne of the Panchen, the second most holy incarnation in Tibet.

It was equally depressing to recall the split between the Dalai Lama, who still looked like a studious undergraduate, and the last Panchen Lama, who had looked like a sulky football player. After a tragic reign as a cat's paw of the Chinese, the last Panchen had died suddenly and inexplicably.

There were now two ostensible Panchen Lamas, both infants. One was the Dalai Lama's selection, the other Beijing's. Kneeling before the great golden image of the Buddha of the Future, Robbie prayed that the divisive quarrel would be resolved by an unmistakable sign from Heaven for the Dalai Lama's candidate.

Lhasa itself, he reflected as the jouncing bus carried him south toward Kathmandu, had been a shocking disappointment. His childhood memory was a city of snug houses and great temples dominated by the soaring Potala, the Dalai Lama's residence. Its master an exile, the immense Potala still stood untouched, its graceful pale yellow facade rising step by step to its layered roofs, which curved upward toward Heaven. Even though he had, like all children, seen all things larger than life, Robbie knew he now beheld a capital that had been violated and broken during the three decades since he had last seen it. Lhasa, too, was dominated by gray blocklike buildings in the graceless modern Chinese style.

The snug houses he remembered had been taken over by Chinese officials, soldiers, and businessmen. Chinese policemen patrolled the city, their haughty manner a constant reminder of Tibet's humiliation, and the streets were thick with Chinese pedestrians. Beijing was rapidly turning Lhasa into a Chinese city by immigration and by births, making Tibetans a minority, virtually intruders in their own capital.

Now, returning to the world outside, Robbie saw in his mind's eyes the slight but erect figure of the matriarch, his father's mother. Her dark eyes flashed when she told him that she had not summoned him solely for the pleasure of seeing him once again before she died. Her necklaces of amber, coral, turquoise, and silver glowing in the wintry dusk that shadowed one of the few substantial houses still in Tibetan hands, she had made her wishes clear. His religion, as well as his personal principles, she had reminded him, required his obedience.

Her voice was sonorous, her rhetoric formal, and her manner portentous—like a prophet revealing a vision: "Our victory, our very survival, must be won on the mattress, matrimonial or not. Tibetans are growing fewer while the Chinese are growing more numerous every day. Already there are five million Chinese to five million Tibetans. And they draw on a reservoir of more than a billion Chinese. Tibetans must fight back."

"Grandmother, I'm doing all I can," Robbie said. "His Holiness orders me to keep him informed on South China and Hong Kong. That's my contribution."

"You could do more, Dorje," she chided. "And what a pleasant way to fight a war! Between a woman's soft thighs! I want you to give me more great-grandsons, lad."

"Of course, Grandmother. But there is an obstacle—"

"Some woman in Hong Kong? *Not* a *Chinese* woman?"

"An American. No, we're not married. But I have an obligation toward her."

"What nonsense!" the old lady snapped. "She is there, and you are here. How can she stop you?"

"I cannot break my word!"

"Have you promised her marriage? No? Then what stops you from doing as I wish?"

When Robbie didn't reply, she continued, "Your elder half-brother died six months ago. His widow, Kukula, is alone. She has need of a man—to protect her and to give her a son."

"But, honored Grandmother, I—"

"You're all but married to Kukula already, lad," the matriarch insisted. "A woman takes all the brothers to husband when advisable. It is now not merely advisable, but essential."

"Grandmother, I've told you—His Holiness wants me to return to Hong Kong. I am most useful there, he—"

"By all means return, Dorje. But first do as I wish. When you leave, your name, as her husband, will protect Kukula. She will remain to give Tibet another warrior. Your woman in Hong Kong you can marry under the law of that pagan place. And you will still be married to Kukula under Buddha's law. How can you possibly object?"

"I have only promised one thing, Grandmother," Robbie remonstrated. "I swore I would not marry in Lhasa, not before talking with her."

"She is there, and you are here," the matriarch repeated. "Your duty to your family far outweighs—cancels—your promise to some loose-moraled foreign tart."

"She is anything but a loose-moraled tart," he objected hotly. "My promise is a matter of personal honor!"

"We'll see about that, Dorje," his grandmother retorted. "Family honor comes before personal honor. Without a family behind you, personal honor is meaningless. You *will* do as you're told."

Two months after playing out that domestic drama, Dorje Rabnet now found himself on the shiny green bus that was creaking and rattling toward Shigatse and, in time, Kathmandu. The land route to Dharamsala and the aerial route to Hong Kong were opening before him—and he was glad. He had found Lhasa not only disappointing, but oppressive.

He loved his motherland, and he would make any sacrifice for Tibet. But to live permanently in Lhasa? No! Not yet at least!

If it were necessary, Robbie assured himself, he would sacrifice himself and his personal happiness for Tibet. Above all beings he reverenced the bodhisattvas who gave up Nirvana in order to help others to attain enlightenment. Like a bodhisattva, he would give up everything to help others, above all, Tibetans. But that sacrifice wasn't necessary. To the contrary, the Dalai Lama, his superior in all matters, spiritual or earthly, had instructed him to return to Hong Kong.

Bracing himself against the bus's swaying and bucking on the rocky road, the senior bodyguard passed Robbie a shiny aluminum thermos bottle filled with strong tea heavily buttered and salted. It was also stiff with tsampa, that Tibetan staple, roasted barley flour. A modern thermos and a medieval concoction, that was Tibet today.

Twilight was falling, and the feeble headlights could hardly pierce the darkness. The small bus was the only vehicle in the wilderness, its occupants the only humans. To the south Robbie could make out the curve of a mountain range, snow-frosted peaks glimmering through the gloom. Closer he saw a landscape of desolation under a dark sky obscured by waves of soiled gray clouds. The dun plain, tinted by pale yellow lichen and dark green moss, stretched endlessly outward from the potholed gravel road.

Behind a string of nondescript hillocks, Robbie sensed as much as saw a half-frozen river glinting eerily in the tarnished light. A half-dozen yakhide coracles were strewn on its shelving banks. The crude round design, eminently practical in a timber-poor land, was unchanged since Noah launched his high-tech ark.

The bus lurched around a long twisting bend, to reveal a lake glistening beneath smoke-gray cliffs. Robbie remembered that precipice from his inward journey and shivered. It looked unearthly cold, frozen as hard as an Arctic glacier.

He shivered and drew over his shoulders the fur cloak his grandmother had given him as a going-away present. He doffed his fedora and pulled down the ear flaps of the fur hat his grandmother had also given him. Perhaps he would not freeze this night.

"Look there! Up ahead!" the driver exclaimed. "What's that?"

Through the thickening gloom Robbie glimpsed feeble headlights shining diagonally across the road. Squinting into the half darkness, he made out a figure in a heavily quilted green overcoat, who was waving a lantern to halt the bus.

As the distance closed rapidly, he saw a high-slung canvas-enclosed jeep. That obsolete Soviet design was still favored by the Chinese People's Liberation Army. The clumsy boxy shape leaning crazily to one side in the dusk terrified him.

Robbie's heart leaped into his throat. His pulse pounded; his breathing was ragged. To have come so far—and now on virtually the last lap!

The driver lifted his foot from the accelerator, and the bus slowed. But a bodyguard shouted, "More gas! Put your foot down!"

The next moment, the second bodyguard exclaimed, "Maybe flat tires, maybe a broken axle. Either way, they can't chase us!"

The Chinese soldier with the lantern dived out of the path of the accelerating bus. Encumbered by his thick quilted overcoat, he was almost swatted like a fly. Unable to believe until the last moment that a Tibetan bus would not halt at his command, he skittered on the ice and fell hard, smashing his lantern.

"More gas!" the bodyguard shouted. "Faster, for Buddha's sake! They'll shoot."

The young driver obeyed, although the steering wheel twitched in his hands like a living thing when the tires spun on the icy gravel. The bus was swaying from side to side, jinking and juddering on the rough, slippery surface, when the first shot spattered the dust. An instant later, an automatic rifle chattered irately.

The passengers dropped to the floor, but the driver was pinned to the steering wheel. Another sharp burst sounded, but it was farther away—and Robbie sighed in relief.

At that moment, the driver slumped in his seat. His hands grudgingly gave up their grip, his nerveless fingers slipping one by one off the slick plastic wheel. He toppled to the steel floorboards, bleeding heavily from a small puncture in his neck.

The bus hurtled ahead, yawing from side to side like a boat in a high sea. The accelerator was jammed down, the battered machinery failing under the strain of full speed.

Defying his fear, Robbie pulled himself from seatback to seatback toward the wheel. The soldiers' automatic rifles were now almost out of range. Yet a final burst shattered the windshield before his eyes. He clung to the seatbacks with both hands.

Tires worn smooth and slick skidded on a patch of ice and lost traction. Virtually floating on the ice, the bus swerved to the left and slid toward the cliffs overlooking the frozen lake.

Robbie hurled himself at the steering wheel, unavoidably treading on the driver. The slick plastic almost slithered out of his cold-numbed fingers. He kicked the jammed accelerator, and it freed itself. He touched the brake gently—and the bus slowed minutely.

Robbie peered through the shattered windshield, his eyes watering in the frigid blast of the wind—and braked frantically. No time to worry about skidding on the ice-rimmed gravel. The cliff's edge was no more than ten feet away. He braked again tentatively, very gently, but the spinning tires were sliding sideways on the sheet ice, beyond all control.

Resigned, he lifted his hands from the useless steering wheel. His thoughts turned to Lucretia with vast regret and profound sorrow—and he murmured a brief prayer.

Unmoving, the distant Chinese soldiers watched in vengeful fascination the angular bus hurtle over the precipice. Driven by its own momentum, it rose in the air, and its headlights feebly probed the gray sky. When it lost momentum, the pale yellow beams gyrated against the dark horizon. The bus arched a graceful parabola against the frigid sky, plunged downward, and spattered on the frozen lake.

A flicker licked out from the gas tank, flared into flame, and exploded into a fireball within a few seconds. The mute signal of the headlights expired, and only the leaping flame of the funeral pyre lit the night. The ice opened, and the blazing bus subsided into the lake. The flames hissed furiously as the water quenched them, but no human ear heard that fierce lament.

A WEEK OR so later, Lucretia was sipping her breakfast coffee and leafing through the *South China Morning Post,* annoyed again by its servile tone toward Beijing. On page five the word *Tibet* caught her eye. She folded the newspaper to read the two-paragraph item at the foot of column three beside a cosmetics ad. Her movements were deliberate and controlled.

Just seeing or hearing the word *Tibet* could nowadays trigger rapid breathing like the onset of a panic attack. She knew there was unlikely to be news of Robbie in a random snippet from a country all but unknown to the world and therefore little reported. But she could not control her spontaneous reaction.

BUS OVER TIBET CLIFF, she read, *all aboard lost*. Lucretia's breathing rasped with anxiety. She scanned the item, which might have something to do with Robbie. The skeletal story reported only that a bus en route from Lhasa to Kathmandu had plunged over a cliff into a lake. Nothing was known regarding the fate of the passengers, who were not identified. An unnamed source in Kathmandu said small-arms fire had been heard by nomads near the site of the accident.

It was stupid, ridiculous, even to think Robbie could be involved, Lucretia told herself. Was she going to tremble at every single last news item about Tibet? Yet he could well be involved. It was long past time for his return, and he could have been a passenger on the doomed bus.

Lucretia's coffee cup clattered against its saucer—not only the harsh rapid breathing, but the trembling hands and the blurred vision. She would certainly succumb to another panic attack if she did not rein in her wild imagination.

With an intense, conscious physical effort, she mastered her treacherous nerves. Idiotic to react so violently to a fragmentary report that was probably wrong! Farfetched to think it could have any connection with Robbie!

She, nonetheless, telephoned acquaintances at Reuters, which had run the item, and the Associated Press, which might know more. The desk man at Reuters was sorry, but that was all he'd received. No, no more was likely to come, no amplification. The woman on the AP desk said she hadn't noticed the item in the *Post* and had seen nothing similar on the wire.

"Too thin for us, I guess, speculative and not terribly important," she added. "Lucretia, you can't worry about every little squib out of Tibet. Robbie'll be back—or he won't—like you've been saying. But he's not a politician or a criminal whose name makes news. So the first you'll know is when he turns up safe and sound."

THE LETTER ARRIVED five days later, its envelope stained and torn. Since the meticulous Hong Kong Post Office rarely, if ever, subjected a letter to mistreatment, the fault must lie with the sender. It bore in black ink the address: *Mrs Lukreshia Barness* and the address. Lucretia tore the envelope open.

Dear Mrs Lukreshia,
Please to accept my kindest wishes for your being ever healthy and growing in wealthiness.

She glanced down at the signature that closed the four paragraphs. Hong Kong Old Lama, she read, and remembered Robbie's speaking of the aged monk who was the elder of the small Tibetan community.

Deeply regretfully must advise you, Mister Dorje Rabnet is perished. His fate had been sealed when he fell off a cliff in a fawlty omnibus. Seven aboard: none lived.
I must tell you because you must never any longer think he is coming back. He will never, never come back to Hong Kong. All very, very sad. We much consolation you, Mrs Barness, madam. We are also sorrowing with you.
Very clear is time for you to go away.
Very sorry and heartfelt
Hong Kong Old Lama
—(by Lee Fokee, public letter writer)

Through the tears that stung her eyelids, Lucretia saw the note under the signature she had almost missed:

Post Scriptum: I, Hong Kong Old Lama, have in my aprropri-ate custodie at 234A Lockhart Road the small lion dog of Mis-ter Rabnet. Do you want this dog?

13

LUCRETIA FELT HERSELF falling through thin air, falling endlessly into a bottomless abyss. Her first overwhelming, irrational reaction had been flat refusal to believe that Robbie had left her forever. No longer denying reality, she was now plunging into the abyss, her grief erupting in hoarse screams.

Ensnared by anguish, Lucretia wept and wailed like a woman of some barbaric desert tribe. Nothing in the world could console her, for nothing any longer had meaning or value for her.

When, exhausted by grief, she lay mute and motionless on her bed, Lucretia's first rational reaction was, quite astonishingly, overwhelming relief. She was now beyond the vain hopes and the harrowing uncertainty, no longer to wonder if he still lived and whether he suffered. It was over, all over now.

She knew that she still cared desperately, still loved Robbie to distraction. Perhaps she always would. But it was all over now—

forever. If only she could believe in a single Christian Heaven or many Tantric Heavens—and look forward to meeting him there someday!

Afterward, she was lapped in the profound serenity of exhaustion, the calm after the storm. Nothing more to expect or to fear, nothing to hope for or to guard against, neither rapture nor heartbreak! The best she could do for Robbie now was to look to her own well-being. That sounded unfeeling even in her own ears. But what else was there? There were no children to rear with love, no family to console in shared grief. There was only Robbie's mother, who was beyond joy and sorrow alike.

Time then to move on—before Hong Kong became hateful to her as the scene of terrible anguish as well as great joy. There was nothing here for her. Anyway, the owners of the apartment were returning after a month or so. With nowhere to live, she would have to move on.

Lucretia was surprised by the calm that succeeded her transports of grief. She suffered no panic attack, although the warning symptoms had roiled her days from Robbie's hasty departure until she learned of his fate. She now went in a businesslike way about the business of discharging the few tasks she could still do for Robbie.

She made an appointment with T. Y. Lee, who surprised her by answering his office phone himself. When she told him her doleful news face-to-face, the old banker was as shaken as he might have been by the death of his own son. His small eyes teared, then dulled. His hands shook, and he blew his nose repeatedly. Only after a minute or two could he speak coherently. The old man then cross-questioned her exhaustively before he was satisfied that nothing could be done. Still, he muttered, "I'll see about making some more inquiries. Though it's a hundred to one I'll learn nothing."

Thereafter, T. Y. Lee was all business, acute for any age, let alone eighty-five. He ticked off on his trembling fingers the tasks still to be done.

"First, of course, Althea. I've reserved her a place at the Mac-Lehose Clinic when the Sanatorium comes down. I have some funds belonging to her. She gave me something to invest years ago—and she's been lucky. Obviously, I had to keep those funds for Althea for an emergency, not use them just to make it less of a burden for Dorje to keep her in the Sanatorium."

Knowing that T. Y. Lee had contributed generously to Althea Rabnet's keep at the Sanatorium, Lucretia smiled at his bankerly reserve. He would never mention his own contributions.

"There's also Dorje's flat. Should bring about two million. I'll see to that. Nothing for you to worry about, my dear. Ah, what a crop of youngsters there would have been if you and Robbie had only . . ."

Leaving the old man to muse on children who would never come into this world, Lucretia bid him good-bye. She also promised to call on him again before she left Hong Kong. She had decided she would for the time being go back to Cambridge, where she would find not only family sanctuary, but friends, diversion, and opportunities to make her own living and her own way.

Then she visited Robbie's apartment for the last time. The grim gray towers made her shudder still, but the bright red neon *Jook* sign of the ground-floor eating shop was harmless, despite the terror it had once aroused. The two-room apartment on the thirty-fourth floor was redolent of dust and disuse. Yet she caught the faint feral scent of their lovemaking—and was pierced again by the pangs of deprivation.

On the coffee table she saw a large yellow writing pad. Robbie's precise handwriting listed the chores he had to do before departing for Tibet. Most were now meaningless: departure and arrival times beside the numbers of airline flights that had months ago flown into history; a reminder to tell his employers that he could not say exactly when he would return from his unpaid leave of absence; a calculation of the interest on a bank loan of HK$25,000 he had evidently secured to finance his trip.

Lucretia's eyes teared at that reminder of how close to the edge he had lived, never complaining. In order to obey the Dalai Lama's command and his grandmother's summons, Robbie had borrowed the equivalent of US$3,000. Even after years of dedicated work, he could not find that relatively small sum out of his own resources.

She smiled wryly, gratified, yet abashed, when she saw the notation: *Explain to L more clearly why I must go.*

Had that been an afterthought, she wondered, or had he attempted to do so? Had he tried to make her understand why he had to obey those orders? And had she been too angry, too self-centered, too immersed in her own feelings even to listen?

But it was all over, and there was no point in postmortems. She shuddered at that word. But, she could not help asking herself: Could I have been more understanding, not so quick to feel hurt, slower to take offense, less ready to condemn?

Of course she could! Just asking those questions answered

them. She scrubbed angrily at the tears trickling down her cheeks. She did not much like what that simple notation told her about herself.

Lucretia blotted her tears, but she was on the verge of weeping again when she saw the notation at the bottom of the pad: *Jacko > Old Lama, 234A Lockhart Road.*

She'd almost forgotten about Jacobus the lion dog, her last living link to Robbie and the past. Devastated by the Old Lama's letter, she had forgotten that its last word asked if she wanted Jacobus.

Lucretia was lanced by guilt again. Robbie would normally have left Jacobus with her. He must have taken the shih-tzu to the Old Lama because he was not sure she would welcome the dog. Robbie had, of course, known how she felt: her anger at his apparent desertion. Yet how could he have believed she would not welcome the lion dog?

That was one more thing she could do—for herself, as well as for Robbie, before she left Hong Kong. No reason why she could not take Jacobus to Cambridge with her. As Robbie had pointed out, he was a small dog, small though great-hearted, just the dog for a small apartment. Jacobus was also perfect for traveling, compact, neither troublesome nor too expensive to fly. He would be a tremendous consolation.

Number 234A Lockhart Road was in the heart of Wanchai, the raunchy, rowdy redlight and nightclub district that was slowly being extinguished by smart shops, skyscraper offices, expensive restaurants, and remodeled apartments. More than any other section of old Hong Kong, Wanchai reflected constantly changing Hong Kong and its cosmopolitan populace. Nightclubs, glitzy tourist restaurants with gold dragons twined around scarlet pillars, and questionable saunas still studded the district made famous by the archetypical whore with a heart of gold, Suzy Wong. But such enterprises were no longer dominant.

The more domesticated Hong Kong of today was reflected by the rows of shops selling household furnishings. From tiles to bathroom fixtures, from appliances to kitchen furnishings, from wallpaper to carpeting, shops offering the same goods were strung out beside each other. Lucretia wondered: Why? For the convenience of shoppers or so that competitors could watch each other?

Searching for 234A Lockhart Road, she encountered a bizarre yet not untypical cross-section of the many types among the Colony's people. On a folding chair sat a pale wizened Chinese who was at least eighty. He wore an embossed white skullcap on his bald head and carried his false teeth in his shirt pocket. He only spoke to quote a ludicrously low price for a shoeshine, and he took half an hour for each patron. Robbie had said the old man's was the best shine he'd ever had.

A Punjabi couple caught her eye. The husband wore phenomenally baggy unpressed white cotton trousers under a loose white shirt that came below his knees. His black beard was a vigorous adornment to a powerful, highly dignified face. His nose growing straight from his forehead might have graced a general of Alexander the Great. Demure in pastel flowered pajamas and an enveloping shawl, his little gray wren of a wife walked ten steps behind, her eyes cast down.

A gold Rolls Royce glided around the corner, just missing the wife. The license was GG 8888, a number highly prized by the superstitious for its promise of even greater prosperity: *baht,* meaning eight, rhymes with *faht,* as in *faht-choi,* meaning get rich.

The rear windows were thickly curtained. The passenger was assuredly a Muslim or Hindu woman in *purdah,* kept from the eyes of any man except her husband and her brothers. That medieval practice in ultramodern, go-go Hong Kong!

Lucretia saw in quick succession: a very dark man, evidently Indian, African, or South Seas islander, his face set like an evil stone idol's, haranguing himself loudly and unintelligibly; a red-haired Chinese boy with a heavy gold chain around his neck and a black satchel over his shoulder, darting from place to place, either delivering small objects or, more likely, soliciting; a blind beggar peddling chewing gum; a mangy dog gnawing on a grapefruit rind; and poor men, who wore only cotton undershirts and worn blue shorts against the dank chill in the air, sleeping the day away under blankets of corrugated cardboard.

Just around the corner, Lucretia remembered, a glittering showroom did a brisk business in Lamborghinis at US$175,000 and up. The contrasts of Wanchai were endlessly fascinating, but she had found 234A. At the foot of a narrow flight of stairs sandwiched between an interior decorator and an old-fashioned noodle shop, Lucretia saw a painted *thanka* showing the Tibetan wheel of life, the stages of the human journey through this world to the next.

That grotesque picture of mankind's fate was the more frightening for the supernatural being behind it. The wheel was propped between the scimitar-nailed feet and the fanged mouth of a dark brown figure with terrifying red eyes and a crown of skulls. Trudging upward, Lucretia smelled incense and a votive butter lamp even before she saw the statuette of the thunderbolt-wielding, blood-dripping black goddess of death and destruction set in a dark niche beside a door protected by a grill barred with five locks.

Superstitious fear would keep the shrine safe. But the grill showed that stronger protection was needed for vulnerable human beings and their paltry treasures.

The gnarled ancient who answered the bell was unmistakably the Hong Kong Old Lama himself. There could not be two such figures in Wanchai, much less in one small apartment. He wore a yellow felt chuba and a necklace of amber beads carved into death's heads. His expression was severe, by no means welcoming.

Lucretia wondered what he thought of her. Certainly disapproval—and probably far worse—because she came from another world and because she had tried to lure Robbie away from this world. Still, he unlocked the grill and curtly waved Lucretia into a red-painted room that was evidently a chapel. On the shelves along the walls stood hundreds of small gilt images of the Buddha. In the better light within the apartment, she also saw that innumerable wrinkles seamed the Hong Kong Old Lama's copper-red face. His thin lips were turned down in distaste, and his black eyes were baleful. For Lucretia, the elderly lama personified the malign aspect of Tantric Buddhism. Robbie had not dwelt on the dark side of his religion, which also worshiped the black goddess of bloodshed and havoc. But she had read about its fearsome rituals.

The Old Lama said not a word. Robbie had told her he spoke no English and precious little Cantonese. Perhaps she should bark like a dog to explain her mission. Unspeaking, the Old Lama opened a door—and Jacobus bounded out. He was uncombed and bedraggled, the sheen gone from his golden hair. He was barking in the shrill falsetto that expressed joy.

It was a raucous, joyous welcome. When the lion dog looked around expectantly, her heart fell. He was looking for Robbie. Jacobus had never seen her without Robbie.

THE RAINY FEBRUARY of 1997 dragged its sodden length across the calendar. Late one overcast afternoon, Lucretia was painting in the bedroom of her hosts' son. The reverse-cycle air conditioner could make little impression on the damp cold preceding the Lunar New Year, not even supplemented by the three-bar heater the British quaintly called an electric fire.

She looked like a plump Chinese doll. Her long cheongsam of gray silk with many-colored flowers embroidered on cuffs, hem, and shoulder opening was padded with bulky raw silk for warmth. At her feet lay a furry golden shape. Now scrubbed and brushed, Jacobus looked like an expensive child's toy, truly a plush animal.

Cocooned in shawls, Lucretia had wrapped a big red and blue apron around herself to protect the cheongsam from the pigments. She did not care if she looked fat, dowdy, and eccentric. For once, she was blessedly warm.

Vivid against a complexion that was stark white in the sun-shy winter, her crow-black hair was piled carelessly on top of her head and negligently skewered with a half dozen big hairpins. That casual style made her look about eighteen. Besides, she wore no makeup except a dash of pink lipstick, and she was concentrating on her painting with the intensity of youth.

She chewed abstractedly on the end of her bush, which bore a dab of scarlet pigment for the flame-of-the-forest tree in the background. Her light-blue eyes focused on the central figures in the canvas: a small white kitten confronting an erect black cobra, its hood distended to flaunt its eye-glass marking.

Certain to touch a sentimental chord, a fluffy kitten was perfect for greeting cards and chocolate boxes. But this innocent kitten was unmistakably doomed as it haplessly invited the great snake to play. More than ever, Lucretia's recent paintings showed a dark bizarre streak.

The doorbell in the kitchen pealed distantly. While Lucretia disentangled herself from her cocoon, the bell pealed again, impatient and imperious.

Jacobus looked up at Lucretia without enthusiasm, but dutifully followed her. He would not let her out of his sight, not only because she represented security, but because he clearly believed she must sooner or later lead him to Robbie.

When she opened the door, a young Chinese in blue coveralls was just about to punch his thumb down on the bell-push for the third time. He smiled broadly and inquired, "Have got leaky tap?"

Jacobus watched incuriously as she pointed out the kitchen faucet. She returned to her painting, knowing the workman would let himself out.

She was always hazy about time when she was working, but an hour or so afterward the doorbell pealed again. Resignedly, Lucretia laid down her brush and threw off her shawls. Glancing at the lion dog, she was startled to see him quivering with eagerness.

Jacobus gallantly allowed her to precede him. But when the bell pealed again, he scratched madly at the door. Puzzled, Lucretia eased it open—and the lion dog flung himself at the shadowy figure outside. His tail, extended straight as a lance, wagged so furiously that it was a blur as Jacobus jumped up to lick the man's hand.

Lucretia's eyes followed the dog, coming to rest on the drawn face of the tall man. He carried a small valise in his left hand, for his right arm was in a black sling. Something about the haggard features was hauntingly familiar, terribly evocative. But the figure itself was growing fuzzy, smoky and indistinct, writhing like a phantasm in a panic attack.

LUCRETIA'S NEXT SENSATION was droplets of water on her face and Jacobus licking her hand. She was sitting in a cane chair in the living room, and the caller was bending over her, a damp washcloth in his hand. Bewildered, she gazed blankly at the illusion for a few seconds, and her head began to whirl again.

"It's me, darling, nobody else." The voice was unmistakably Robbie's. "Don't faint on me again. What kind of welcome is that?"

She reached out, hardly daring to believe. She reached out and gently touched his face with her fingertips. He was solid flesh and blood and bone, not a hallucination conjured up by her need.

"They . . . they told me you were dead," she faltered. "I thought you were surely dead. Oh, Robbie, it *is* you . . . yourself and alive."

"As ever!" His smiled faded, and he demanded, "Who told you I was dead? You had my letters and messages! How could you believe I was dead?"

"But they said so . . . mostly the Old Lama . . . really only the Old Lama. . . . Oh, my darling, it's unbelievable—glorious. Like being given a new life."

She pulled him to her, and they kissed fiercely.

"Now," she said, "I *know* you're you. No one else could . . . but why did you never telephone—from India or even before coming up here today?" Her hands went to her hair. "I must look a mess."

"Stupidly, I couldn't remember the phone number. So I came to you as fast as I could."

"Letters and messages, you said?" she asked. "I got no letters, no messages. Oh, Robbie, I was so sure you were gone forever."

"They were all sent through the Old Lama. I couldn't know where you might move. But he could find out easily. And from Lhasa it was easier—more convenient and more secure—to send letters to a lama, rather than a foreigner, by the underground's couriers. . . . So *he* told you I was dead! I'll deal with him, I promise you."

"Robbie, you must tell me everything, where you were and what you did. Every minute of it. Your arm, what's wrong? Is it broken?"

"Almost healed now."

"You don't look well, not at all," she said. "But why should the Old Lama stop your letters? And say you were dead? How could anyone be so cruel to someone he'd never even met?"

"It's clear enough, Lucretia. He wanted you gone—far away from Hong Kong. So you couldn't get in the way of his plan to marry me to his niece. To keep me wholly Tibetan—in the family."

Jacobus was watching Robbie with adoration. His tail flopped softly against the chair as if to tell Lucretia: See, I told you he'd come back to us. But his eyes were asking Robbie reproachfully: How could you leave me? I'll never let you go again.

Lucretia grasped Robbie's arm to reassure herself again that he was real, not an apparition. He grimaced, and she relaxed her grip. Selma Lotz had told her to hang on to him, but not so hard perhaps. She held his hand tight while he told her the story of the missing months.

Smiling, he concluded, "The Khampas, our nomadic bandit-patriots, wiped out the Chinese troops stranded beside their broken-down jeep. Then the Khampas found me. They looked after me till I could travel again. I got across the border with my pilgrim documents. And that was that."

"The bus went over the precipice, landed in the lake," she persisted. "How could you get out?"

"I couldn't! I didn't! My bodyguard was astonishing, a superman. He smashed the door open and flung me out seconds before the water began pouring in."

"So he saved both of you?"

"He didn't save himself. He couldn't. It was one or the other—and he chose me."

"It's a miracle, a true miracle! You may make a believer of me yet," Lucretia half-bantered, but then asked, "Robbie, what did your grandmother want?"

He had thought about that inevitable question, but had not quite worked out his answer. Only the truth, he now saw, would do. The truth, but not necessarily *all* the truth.

"As you suspected, not just to see me. My half-brother'd died of TB. I never knew him, Lucretia. Grandmother wanted me to marry his widow, Kukula. She said I was in effect already married to Kukula. As you know, a woman often marries all the brothers. It's an old Tibetan . . . an old family custom."

"Not in this family, my boy! Remember that!" she instructed

playfully. "What'd you do? How'd you handle it? You're not married to this Kukula?"

"No, I'm not married to Kukula."

"Anyway, what was she like? Was she very attractive? Did you like her?"

Not *all* the truth. He would certainly not mention his grandmother's pressing him to sleep with Kukula.

"She wasn't terribly attractive," he replied simply. "I didn't want to get too close to her. Like almost everybody in Tibet, she smelled of rancid yak butter! Only more so!"

14

JACOBUS SHOULD HAVE been with them, though it would have taken a pot full of shinbones to divert the shih-tzu every time they wanted privacy. Still, he really should have been with them, rather than staying with Selma Lotz. He belonged with them, but red tape had kept them from taking the shih-tzu from British Hong Kong to Portuguese Macau forty-five miles away. Anyway, they'd left in a hurry and would only be away three days.

Robbie said shih-tzus were wonderful with children, gentle and protective. Lucretia intended to test that statement just as soon as she could. She was not dreaming of a half-dozen children like some ambitious twenty-year-old. But three would not be too many, not if they got right to it. They better had. Thirty-three wasn't too old to begin a family nowadays, but it wasn't twenty, either.

They were certainly doing their best during this blessed interlude at the nineteenth-century Bela Vista Hotel. She smiled again at the shinbones that would have been needed to keep Jacobus from disturbing them. She hadn't told Robbie that she was no longer taking precautions or that this was her most fertile time. Whatever they decided about their future together, she was determined to have his child. All she needed was a little luck.

Lucretia felt guilty. Not for the great love between them or for making love without benefit of clergy or sanction of the state. Their lovemaking was even more joyous and exhilarating, more poignant as well, for the grim interval when he had wondered if he would ever return and she had believed he would never return. She felt guilty about the amount of money they were spending.

"What, squander all that lolly?" had been his first reaction when she suggested this brief holiday. Even at a preferential rate, three days at the Bela Vista cost more than US$800 plus food and incidentals. That was just about all the cash they could scrape up between them. When they got back to Hong Kong, they'd have only a few dollars in their bank accounts, and Robbie had to pay back the HK$25,000 borrowed for his journey to Tibet. Though the Dalai Lama's secretary had spoken of recompensing him, nothing had yet appeared.

Somehow, though, she'd talked him into going to Macau. They both needed a break from dank, depressing Hong Kong, and he still didn't look well.

The weather in Macau was, of course, much the same as in Hong Kong. But the atmosphere was different. Despite a recent rash of building, Macau was still visibly rooted in the more leisurely past, rather than the hectic present. In Macau, they could talk seriously about their future, as they could not in Hong Kong, where they were plagued by too many memories and too many interruptions.

At midweek the Bela Vista was blissfully quiet, all but deserted. Detached from the workaday world, it was the ideal place to spend three days out of time. Yet it would be crammed with guests next week when swarms flocked from Hong Kong to celebrate the Lunar New Year by betting in Macau's casinos. The gambling halls were the temples of Hong Kong's secular religion of greed. Roulette, fan tan, and hi-lo were its solemn rites.

The Bela Vista was, however, dedicated to the rites of graceful living, having been a hotel on and off for more than a century. Its three stories with their pillared verandas were now resplendent in immaculate pale yellow picked out with white. Its eight suites were opulently furnished, and old-fashioned claw-footed bathtubs big enough for two dominated the capacious bathrooms with ultramodern plumbing.

Old-timers remembered when the Bela Vista was a blotched, peeling poison-green, its interior battered and its plumbing grumbling. Even then, this oldest hostelry in the oldest European enclave on the China coast had exerted a singular charm. It was today one of those frivolous yet beautiful jewels that hard-headed, rapacious, twentieth-century capitalism occasionally spawns, much as a jagged, barnacled oyster spawns a pearl.

Wholly relaxed for the first time in nearly a year, Robbie already looked better. He had conceded, "It's a wild extravagance, but it's worth it."

From time to time, Lucretia caught him gazing at her as if afraid she would vanish. Otherwise, he was visibly unwinding.

His face was losing the sickly yellow cast of high altitude sunburn and returning to its normal ruddy amber. His eyes again shone jade-green, no longer shadowed by fear and anxiety. His hollowed cheeks were filling out as the imaginative cuisine restored the pounds he'd lost in Tibet. He was again the old Robbie she loved, though surely a little wiser and perhaps a little more tolerant of both her foibles and his own.

His only complaint was the lack of a pool. Robbie loved to swim—to the astonishment of his Tibetan friends, who looked on water in any guise as either toxic or a man-trap. He'd learned from the ubiquitous Billy Tingle, a short, muscular man who'd taught generations of Hong Kong's foreign children to swim. On Saturdays, Tingle had presided over calisthenics and cricket for hundreds of solemn little boys in white shorts and pert red-and-white caps on the broad lawns of the Cricket Club beside the old Bank of China building.

That weekly spectacle had reminded compulsive Hong Kong that life offered joys other than making money. The Cricket Club grounds were a green park in the Central District, the most expensive land in the world. The Club had long since made way for still more office buildings, and the Bank of China now occupied the brutal glass tower on the hillside a few hundred yards away.

Instead of swimming, Robbie took long walks through Macau arm in arm with Lucretia. Ignoring the persistent drizzle, they walked for hours, and they talked intermittently. In their little suite they made love for hours, and they talked and talked. Not the chit-chat of acquaintances nor the ardent promises of new lovers. They talked about themselves and the future.

"I can now see the rabbit in the moon clearly," Lucretia declared. "And you could always see the man in the moon. So we're not that different!"

"Different enough!" he responded. "But not totally different. Just different enough to attract each other and then stick together—like the opposite poles of magnets."

"Robbie, this rift in our lives while you were away . . . I see you differently now. But I still love you just as . . . No, I love you more. When I thought you weren't coming back—not ever—I learned how much I need you."

"I didn't have much time to think," he mused. "When I wasn't dodging the Chinese, I was telling stay-at-home Tibetan chieftains about a world they couldn't begin to imagine. Or fighting Grandmother's pressure to marry. Sometimes though, I saw you in my mind's eye. And I remembered how beautiful and quick and humorous and . . . and just how wonderful you were! I now see I was mistaken."

"Mistaken about what?" she laughed. "You can always call it off, the whole thing, if . . ."

"I was badly mistaken," he smiled slyly. "You're more beautiful, more acute, more wonderful than I could ever imagine."

"I was wrong about you, too. I thought you were a tower of strength, fixed and unshakable. I thought you were a solid foundation to build a life on. I thought you'd make up for my flightiness, my impulsiveness."

"And?"

"You'll do fine as a foundation. But I've discovered you're impulsive, too. Almost as impulsive as me."

Resolved to clear up all their differences, she continued all but accusingly, "You didn't have to go off half-cocked. You didn't have to jump on the next plane to India as if there'd never be another. You could've put it off one more day. And you could've tried even harder to get it into my thick head why you had no choice. Why you *had* to go, just as if they'd tied you up and thrown you on the plane."

"Perhaps I could've put it off another day. But I was afraid. If I didn't go immediately, if I saw you again, I feared, I might never leave."

"And you couldn't have lived with yourself, or with me, if I'd kept you from going." She trailed her fingertips across the back of his hand. "Anyway, if you hadn't gone, I'd never've thought so hard about . . . about us. About being together for a long, long time."

"Where'd it get you, that deep thinking? What'd you learn? The same as I did?"

"I don't know exactly what you learned, what you decided. But I learned I'd have to be less self-centered, not so hypersensitive, if it were to work for us. I also concluded we *could* make a go of it. Lots of couples have a lot less in common."

"Lucretia, I've learned I'm truly a Tibetan, but not *all* Tibetan. With a little slack, a little, maybe a lot of, mutual tolerance, we can surely make a go of it. God knows, this . . . this . . ."

"Say it, darling. Say it loud: this great love that binds us . . ."

"Yes, this great love. God knows, it's strong enough, like a steel cable. It'll keep us together. No doubt about that."

"You know, Robbie, my love, we don't *have* to get married. Only pledge to each other we won't part. Lots of people nowadays—"

"It's not that. I'm not afraid of marrying." He grinned broadly. "Marrying you, that's a great idea. But there's the same old fly in the ointment: Hong Kong. I want to stay, have to stay. But you want to go."

"You're saying there's no point in marrying if you're living in

Hong Kong and I in Cambridge? Robbie, it doesn't have to be make-or-break. I'd like to give it a try here—if you'll remember that Hong Kong's *not* the whole known world."

"Let's be honest. Even if I could work somewhere else, even if His Holiness decides I'm no longer needed here . . . there's my mother. If I'm not here to look after her . . ."

"Althea doesn't even recognize you now. All those months, you know, I went to see her once a week. And not a peep out of her about you. You're away for months, and, I hate to say it, she doesn't miss you. How could she? She only needs someone, almost anyone, just to sit with her."

Robbie was silent, depressed by that melancholy truth.

"She has a lot of visitors," Lucretia resumed. "I bumped into them all the time. She must have been wonderful, your mother, to have so many devoted friends still. But, sadly, you're now just another visitor to her."

"I see!" He hated to acknowledge that in reality his mother had already left him. "But it's not so easy. I have to be here to pay for her. The MacLehose Clinic'll cost a fortune, more than twice what I'm paying at the Sanatorium."

"I *am* sorry, Robbie. I've been so happy I just forgot to tell you T. Y. Lee had some money of Althea's. And his bank'll look after the payments if he dies. To make doubly sure she has enough, why not sell your apartment? It'll easily fetch two million Hong Kong."

"Hold on now. Sell the flat and where would I . . . we . . . live? It's still Hong Kong, and housing's still sky high."

"I've been asking around the Chinese University. I'm not just talking through my hat about staying for a while. They can use me full time next semester. A two-bedroom apartment is part of the deal."

"I see," he said slowly. "You're dead earnest, aren't you?"

"Of course!"

He took her hand in his and said, "I'm meant to get down on my knees, to be passionate and tender or, at least, clever and witty. But I can only ask: Do you mean you will—if I beg you, plead with you—you *will* marry me?"

"Robbie, darling, you don't have to plead or be witty. I told you I've been doing some deep thinking. Of course I will."

"I'm no longer surprised," he burbled. "Only delighted! Overjoyed! Overwhelmed! Champagne, darling? Caviar?"

"Yes, please," said Lucretia.

The Pommery arrived so fast the staff must have anticipated their exuberant order. When they'd finished the caviar and were sipping the second bottle of Pommery, Lucretia, the romantic, not Robbie, the pragmatic, returned to the practical issue.

"Then you'll leave your apartment on the market, just in case? And I'll tell the vice-chancellor yes?"

"Let's see what we get," he agreed. "I'll have to put aside most of it for Mum. Whether we stay or go, she's got to be protected."

"Certainly, darling. Just keep enough for airplane tickets to . . . to wherever. Then we can pool our talents—and our poverty."

"You know," he mused. "I can afford to test the waters after June 1997. I can—"

"They'll be rough waters," she interjected.

"Of course," he replied. "But they can't keep me from leaving if I want to. I'm not Chinese, and my passport's British. Full

British, not a trashy British Overseas National passport that doesn't even entitle you to live in Britain. And if we decide to stay, I was born here. Let Beijing chew on that one!"

Each felt the other was all but persuaded. Lucretia had agreed to remain after June 30, while Robbie was no longer set on staying indefinitely. Yet neither was completely satisfied. That difference was a good basis for a compromise that would actually work.

Because both Lucretia and Robbie still harbored some private doubts, they were both determined to strive to keep the relationship intact. Both therefore believed with justice that they were starting all over again with a far better chance than the average couple just starting out in blissful ignorance.

STILL EXHILARATED, LUCRETIA and Robbie boarded the hydrofoil for Hong Kong the next evening. As always, Robbie found seats near the exit. He almost missed out. The hydrofoil was jammed, every seat occupied.

Even before they cleared the breakwater, the wind whined petulantly and shook the craft. When the hydrofoil rose on its skis outside the breakwater, the wind dropped, and the passengers slumped back into their hard seats.

The fog grew thicker as they drew away from Macau, but the lights were bright inside the closed cabin. From time to time, a gust battered the flying hull, almost unnoticeable in the cabin. The hydrofoil was initially more stable when riding on its skis than with its hull in the water, even with the waves rising. Still, the prudent captain dropped his normal speed of fifty miles an hour to forty.

Familiar with hydrofoils because of his many trips to the outlying islands, Robbie frowned at that reduction in speed. He almost questioned a passing crewman, but did not want to alarm Lucretia. Still, he was uneasy.

After ten minutes of uneventful progress, Robbie relaxed again. Reminding himself that not he, but an experienced crew was responsible for the craft, he took Lucretia's hand.

He almost missed the impact. It was quick, almost passing, and it was light, almost glancing. He noticed the minor collision belatedly, but was not greatly alarmed when the vessel slowed further.

Minutes later the hydrofoil stopped abruptly, subsided into the water, and began rocking violently. When the engine's vibration stopped, Robbie reached under his seat for an orange life vest. He handed it to Lucretia, saying softly, "Put it on, just in case!" He then found another for himself under her seat. Both were standing when the mass of the passengers began to scream and sob.

"Do not be alarmed!" a metallic loudspeaker urged. "We appear to have hit a large object, but the crew are well trained in emergencies. Do not panic! All will be well."

The door to the narrow deck outside was opened by a sweating crewman, and the stench of oil blew into the cabin. Following Robbie, Lucretia was through the door in an instant. She kicked off her high-heeled shoes for better balance on the slippery hull, which was already listing heavily. The fog was thinner now, pierced for a few dozen yards by the blazing cabin lights. An instant later, all the lights went out, leaving them in darkness.

Lucretia was pummeled by the bodies of the fearful passengers swarming out of the cabin and almost fell. Robbie caught her and said into her ear, "I'll lower you as far as I can. When I let go, you're going to get very wet. Swim as far from the vessel as you can. Don't wait an instant."

"And you?" she shouted over the cries of the throng. "What about you?"

"I'll follow you. I know these hydrofoils."

Grasping her hands hard, Robbie let her down gradually. When his grip slowly relaxed, she clung desperately, as if safety lay in the sinking vessel, rather than the water. Her fingers slipped through his—and she was falling. She dropped into the waves, plunged under the surface, and choked on greasy salt water. The buoyant life vest popped her up again, and she spat out the water.

It was not as bad as she had feared. The life vest kept her bobbing above the surface, sliding up the sides of the waves and dropping down into the troughs. The fog was now much thinner, and she saw the searchlights of another vessel approaching rapidly. The radioman had obviously sent out distress calls.

The newcomer slowed near the sinking hydrofoil and approached gingerly. Its searchlights alternately played on the sinking vessel and probed the waves for swimmers. Each time the lights swept the hull, Lucretia looked frantically for Robbie. But she did not see him or, if she did, she could not distinguish him among the throng floundering into the water.

Lucretia reassured herself. He was a practiced swimmer and was, as he had reminded her, familiar with hydrofoils. She blew the whistle attached to the life vest and shouted at the top of her voice.

In almost instant reply, she felt herself lifted out of the water, dangling like an unwieldy puppet from a boathook. Reaching out, she grasped a rope hanging down the side of the second hydrofoil—and was borne upward to the narrow deck.

Lucretia gazed at the stricken vessel, its deck now bright with the searchlights of still a third hydrofoil. In that artificial daylight she glimpsed Robbie. He was clinging to a cleat on the sharply canted deck, helping others into the inflated rubber rafts now congregating around the sinking hull.

Lucretia smiled pridefully. He would, of course, do so. Not only had he kept his head, but he was now helping others. She was only slightly disturbed, only a little anxious at his potentially dangerous altruism. Really though, there was no longer any danger. He would be taken aboard one of the rescue craft when he was ready. She could not realistically expect that it would be the one on which she was now safe.

Reassured, she allowed herself to be led into the crammed cabin of the rescue vessel. It lingered for another half hour, evidently to ensure that all were saved. Then it rose onto its skis and pointed its sharp nose toward Hong Kong. The fog had all but dissipated, and she could see the brilliant pyrotechnic display that was the Crown Colony glittering in the distance.

She was helped onto the dock by an attentive sailor, safe again on the land. If only Robbie were with her, it would be a perfect textbook rescue. Anyway she would certainly find him now or later in the arrival hall under the twin red-framed towers of the hydroport.

More anxious, Lucretia fended off policemen and St. John's Ambulance crews eager to bundle her off to a hospital for examination. Having given her name to the clerks who were drawing up lists of the rescued, she waited in hope for more than an hour, while other passengers swept past her.

Looking down, she saw that she was wringing her hands, intertwining and twisting her fingers like a soprano in a tragic opera. She sharply told herself to stop being self-indulgent. She would not give way to despair. She would not!

Naturally, Robbie would be among the last to appear. He would have remained as long as was necessary to help the others.

He would behave like the bodhisattvas he idolized. The most holy souls had sworn not to enter Nirvana "until every blade of grass attains enlightenment." He, too, would unhesitatingly sacrifice himself for others.

Sacrifice himself? She shuddered and thrust the thought away from her. For a skillful swimmer like Robbie, what need could there be to sacrifice himself?

She nonetheless felt a spurt of anger. Why had he not followed her immediately? Why had he abandoned her?

But he had said it himself ages ago: *I could not love thee, dear, so much, loved I not honor more!*

Robbie was as he was, and she loved the man he was!

When the last stragglers had left the hall, a bulky police inspector with a kind Cantonese face approached her.

"About time to go, madam," he said. "There'll be no more coming."

"No more? Are you sure, absolutely sure?"

"I'm afraid so. Maybe your friend, whoever you're looking for, left earlier. We could check with the tally clerks."

The clerks searched the long lists written in spiky letters and scrawled Chinese characters. But no Dorje Rabnet had been recorded.

Meekly acquiescent, Lucretia allowed herself to be taken to Queen Mary Hospital for a cursory examination. Afterward, she found a taxi to take her back to her apartment. It was only nine-thirty in the evening, and the apartment was the best place for her. Robbie would not forget the telephone number this time. When he came ashore, just as soon as he could, he would telephone. His rescuers might have taken him back to Macau, or even to China.

AFTER TWENTY-FOUR sleepless hours, Lucretia had to face the possibility. She could still hope, though feebly, and she could pray to whatever gods existed, as she had last time, when Robbie vanished to Tibet. But she could no longer hope with any confidence after another day passed. Deliberately or not, Robbie must indeed have sacrificed himself for others like a bodhisattva.

No! Not deliberately! How could he have made that choice when they were again so happy together? Not when the future was so bright before them!

Not consciously! Not deliberately! He had simply followed the course that was inevitable, given his noble nature—and he had been consumed by fate.

The idyll was over for good! Lucretia heard the tolling of funeral bells. The idyll was over forever!

The gods had acted, mysteriously and peremptorily as always. Perhaps Buddha the Merciful for his own inscrutable reasons. Perhaps the Old Testament God of Wrath, who had so puzzled Robbie by His jealousy of all other gods.

Whatever gods there were had reached out and swept Robbie away with a negligent flick of a wave. They had left her alive to weep silently—beyond hope, almost beyond despair. They had left her to weep and to cry out incredulously, demanding to know why he had been taken.

No one answered.